Concept and Character in the Barsetshire Novels of Angela Thirkell

**Edited
by
Penelope Fritzer**

**The Angela Thirkell Society
North America**

Copyright © 2005, The Angela Thirkell Society
North America
First published 2005
The Angela Thirkell Society
North America
PO Box 7109
San Diego, CA 92167

Printed in the United States of America
by Sabina Krewsun, American Index, 1050 Pioneer Way, El Cajon, CA.619-442-8788

LIBRARY OF CONGRESS
CATALOGING-IN-PUBLICATION DATA

ISBN 0-9768345-0-2 (pbk)

1. Title. Character and Concept in the Barsetshire Novels of Angela Thirkell.
2. Editor. Penelope Joan Fritzer

Introduction

Angela Thirkell was a novelist whose work appealed to the reading masses until her death in 1960, but eventually that work went through a period of relative oblivion, with many of her books out of print for some years. After Pyramid's brief experiment with publishing some of the Barsetshire novels as romance novels in the 1970s, her books began to be published again in the 1980s by Carroll & Graf, and then in the 1990s through the present by Moyer Bell, which has re-published nearly all of them. This re-publication came about in part through the efforts and lobbying of the Angela Thirkell Society and the Angela Thirkell Society North America, which have also been instrumental in publishing some minor works and autobiographical works by Thirkell, her family, and her friends. The two groups have also kept alive Thirkell's reputation through sponsoring conferences about her, and they have helped to spread her new popularity through collecting references to her and her work and through informal criticism and analysis published in their respective journals, the *Journal of the Angela Thirkell Society* in Britain and the *Bulletin of the Angela Thirkell Society* in the United States.

The present volume is a collection of criticism, assembled and supported by the Angela Thirkell Society North America, about the Barsetshire novels, and it contains work by both academics and lay readers. Hazel Bell has argued previously in "Coronation Summer and After: Angela Thirkell's 'Extra Books' " that the non-Barsetshire books are, with the exception of *Ankle Deep* and *O, These Men, These Men*, far more reflective of Thirkell's abilities and tastes than are the Barsetshire novels. But it was Barsetshire that caught and held her reading public, and Barsetshire that created the loyalty of thousands of readers

i

who avidly followed Thirkell's evocation of comfortable English country life, even through the Depression, World War II, and the unsettled postwar years of continued rationing and political upheaval.

Because of both Thirkell's original wide reading public and the current revival of interest in her work, Barsetshire has become an established literary place of the imagination, one that acts as a signifier of social mores presented with extreme sardonic wit. Although Thirkell borrowed the idea of Barsetshire from Anthony Trollope, she made it her own. Her career of writing about Barsetshire lasted far longer than did Trollope's and she wrote far more about this fictionalized world than did he. Thirkell's twentieth-century Barsetshire novels could not have endured as simple pastiches of Trollope's nineteenth-century work. Rather, Thirkell built upon Trollope's work and expanded it greatly, bringing to her twentieth-century Barsetshire her own inimitable brand of world view, politics, satire, mockery, idiosyncratic use of language, and literary reference, which make her Barsetshire novels a rich trove of material for critics and readers alike.

This book of refereed criticism, *Concept and Character in the Barsetshire Novels of Angela Thirkell*, concentrates for the most part on Thirkell's Barsetshire novels, examining various books for various components. Indeed, it is interesting to see how the different writers, working independently, often identify similar themes. For example, the World War II novels have attracted the attention of the most critics (Stone, Childrey, Minogue, Lenckos, Leffler, and Taylor), their interest provoked perhaps by Barsetshire in wartime as a natural complement to contemporary life during the current war in Iraq. Other writers have chosen to hone in on the attributes of particular characters, such as

Barbara Houlton's examination of Jessica Dean and Aubrey Clover and my own essay on Geoffrey Harvey, or on abstract qualities such as the concept of "home" explicated by Jay Strafford. Use and control of language are the focus of other articles, such as those by Mary Faraci and Susan Kurjiaka, while Jerri Chase investigates equally well-loved writers contemporary to Thirkell, and Cynthia Snowden, like Hazel Bell before her, examines some [other] of Thirkell's literary references. Whatever the subject, the authors included here have been selected because they shine the light of analysis on Thirkell and on Barsetshire.

Because the Barsetshire novels were published first by Hamish Hamilton (in Great Britain), then by Alfred Knopf (in the United States), then partially by both Pyramid and Carroll & Graf, then by Moyer Bell (not yet complete), there are as a result numerous editions, and, because the novels were so long out of print, it is difficult to assemble an entire collection by either Knopf or Hamilton (whose copyrights have been taken over by Penguin). As a result, the writers collected here have used various editions, but have carefully documented them. The reader looking for references, then, is advised to check the Works Cited at the end of each essay, which will clearly indicate the specific edition used and will point the reader in the right direction to find any specific reference cited within any of the Barsetshire novels.

Penelope Fritzer
Coral Springs, Florida
2005

Foreword

The Angela Thirkell Society North America is pleased to present this publication of literary analysis of its eponymous author, Angela Thirkell. A large number of devoted readers follow her chronicles of the families of Barsetshire through the years before and after World War II, and welcome comment on her body of published work. The academic community provides here a thoughtful analysis of Thirkell's topics, concepts and characters, and Society members who are scholars of the intricacies of her work provide an interesting counterpoint to the often more formal academic perspective.

This collection, of course, builds on the novels themselves, but also on many background works available: *Ethnicity and Gender in the Barsetshire Novels of Angela Thirkell* by Penelope Fritzer, *English Country Life in the Barsetshire Novels of Angela Thirkell* by Laura Collins (who introduced many Florida Atlantic University faculty to Angela Thirkell), and *Going to Barsetshire* by Cynthia Snowden are examples of three of these works. *The Dictionary of Angela Thirkell's Barsetshire Novels*, written by Johnny Pate and published by the Angela Thirkell Society, has provided a reference for many of these works. We are particularly indebted to Dr. Fritzer for her efforts to bring this publication to fruition, and to the many contributors from our North American ranks. The publication was made possible through generous contributions by the members of the Angela Thirkell Society. It is a hope and expectation that another volume will be published, and that a wide array of both members and outside scholars again will have an opportunity to participate.

There are many people in the Society who have made this work possible, and the Society would like to acknowledge Edith Jeude, Janet Schmelzer, Phyllis Croghan, Vera Jordan, and the current board: myself, Susan Krzywicki, Kathy Fish, and many others who enable the work of the Society to continue. The Society is especially fortunate to have Deborah Conn, who provides original artwork for this book and for the *Bulletin of the Angela Thirkell Society*. We also thank Janet Schmelzer and Carol Stone for their generous copy editing of this volume and other works. We are very privileged to have our cover designed by Andrew Binder, MFA, of Florida Atlantic University, a fine artist as well as graphic artist and book designer.

Certainly the influence of the "parent" Angela Thirkell Society in England needs to be acknowledged for its generous sharing of Angela Thirkell works and original materials. The current officers, June Cox, Penny Aldred, Jane LeCluse, Edith Fearne, and of course Kate Thirkell, have all been extremely helpful. Society members in the UK, Hazel Bell and Margot Strickland, have also contributed significantly to the body of Angela Thirkell work, Hazel Bell in the area of un-attributed quotations and in indexing issues, and Margot Strickland with her biography, *Angela Thirkell, Portrait of a Lady Novelist.*

And to the many readers of this volume, welcome to an entertaining, educational, and enlightening reading experience. It is the Society's best hope that you enjoy these works as much as the contributors enjoyed preparing them for you.

Barbara Houlton
Angela Thirkell Society North America
2005

Acknowledgements

Deborah Conn's black-and-white drawings appear in a number of newsletters locally and nationwide. She is a watercolor artist as well, and her paintings are shown in many juried shows in Northern Virginia and Maryland. Deborah has a degree in English from Tufts University and, along with her painting, works as a freelance writer and editor She is a member of the Potomac Valley Watercolorists, the Art League, and the Miniature Painters, Sculptors & Gravers Society. When she's not painting or drawing, she's probably reading - Angela Thirkell as well as a wide range of other authors.

Andrew Binder has extensive experience in book cover design and specialized art books. He earned his Master of Fine Arts degree from the University of Miami and has taught both art and technology there and at Lynn University, Palm Beach Community College, and Florida Atlantic University, where he is the webmaster for the College of Education. He is also an accomplished artist who has been shown extensively in South Florida.

TABLE OF CONTENTS

Cheerfulness Breaks In and *Peace Breaks Out* : Bookending World War II
by
Carol Stone

The Barsetshire books of Angela Thirkell are not only a source of pleasure and amusement, but illumine a particular period in the history of England: the time between 1933 and 1960. The years from 1933 - 1939 were part of that era between the wars so well described as "The Long Weekend" in the book of the same name by Robert Graves. The elegant comedy of manners, *The Brandons*, with a surface of exquisite clarity and with no apparent murky depths, appeared in 1939. No subsequent year could have supported this book, since rumours of war and war itself were to follow closely.

The very next book, *Cheerfulness Breaks In*, published in 1940, opens with much the same light-heartedness as *The Brandons*. The frivolous and empty-headed Rose Birkett has become engaged to Lieutenant John Fairweather, a former old boy of Southbridge School, and the wedding is imminent. But there are portents of the storms which already are lowering over Europe. "If there is any trouble about" says Lieutenant Fairweather, "I shall get a special license and marry Rose out of hand" (18). This nervous tone is immediately offset, Thirkell being Thirkell, by the dry comment:

Mr. Birkett's first impulse on hearing that he need not fear that his lovely daughter would be left on his hands,

1

was to say 'Thank God,' but as Headmasters have to keep up a pretence of being slightly more than human he merely said that he hoped things wouldn't be as bad as that (18)

In the usual activities for the time of year, the school's prize-giving and breaking-up take place, and boys head off for the usual locations, without reference to the gloomier prognostications of various politicians. So they disperse for southern France, walking tours of Scandinavia, etc. The reader is introduced again to Lydia Keith, of whom Thirkell says that she "had toned down a little from her schoolgirl days" but promptly reports that Lydia's family "had thought that when she left school she might wish to train for some sort of work in which swashbuckling is a desirable quality, though they could hardly think of any form of employment, short of Parliament, that would give Lydia's powers sufficient scope" (20).

As the party assembles for the wedding, Philip Winter and Lieutenant Fairweather talk about whether there will be "a scrap," and Everard Carter notes that "If anything did happen," he would be continuing his work as a Housemaster with the additional burden of taking on the Hosiers' Boys' Foundation School, thus making it clear that while no one is admitting to the probability of war, contingent plans have certainly been made (25-26). The young women who are bridesmaids are quite forthcoming; Octavia Crawley says that "if there was a war or anything she would drive an ambulance and then she needn't go to dinner parties in the Close, but she knew there would be no such luck" (31). This thread of anxiety and tension continues to appear, culminating at the end of the wedding day when Laura Morland says to Amy Birkett without any euphemisms, that "if there is a war, I will come to you" (*Cheerfulness Breaks In* 61).

The "phony war" which lasted from September 1939 until May 1940 is described by Thirkell with her usual acidic wit in terms of the settling in of the Hosiers' Boys' Foundation School in Southbridge - a settling which involves a great deal of accommodation on the part of all the masters in large part because of the great gulf between classes – and *of the tedium at the Barchester Infirmary where Delia Brandon and Octavia Crawley are working as V. A. D. s with far too little to occupy them. The evolving relationship between Noel Merton and Lydia Keith is interwoven with the activities of the villages of Northbridge and Southbridge, of which Thirkell proves to be an extremely astute observer. Thirkell's description of the working party at Mrs. Keith's at which Mrs. Morland and Mrs. Birkett appear - including the appearance of the revolting Mrs.Warbury - is a case in point.

With only a few words Thirkell evokes the scene, the interactions, and the various characters, sketching an unforgettable picture of the English community as it settles itself in the first months of the war. Naturally she cannot perform this sketch without continuing what she does so very well, gently mocking both the characters and the society. How refreshing this must have been to her readers during the War, who not only had to endure all the difficulties of the war itself but also were continually being urged by their leaders to Keep a Stiff Upper Lip and Not Let the Side Down and other such patriotic verbiage. It must have been a great relief to have something as relatively frivolous as a new Angela Thirkell novel come into one's hands, a novel that reflected the life of the times, but at the same time offered the great relief of laughter.

Such delicious and irrelevant descriptions as the bath which the Arabins had put in about 1876, which was "a massive affair in a heavy mahogany surround with a battery of taps called Sitz, Douche, Plunge and other ominous names, hitting the unwary visitor full in the tenderer parts of his (for no lady visitor ever used it) anatomy with jets of water sometimes scalding, sometimes ice cold" must have provided wartime England with an enthralling and delightful escape from the tedium and fear of daily wartime life (*Cheerfulness Breaks In* 126). Working parties, Red Cross parties, sewing parties of one kind and another, evacuees and the constricting lack of petrol which as the war went on would isolate the Barsetshire communities from one another, were the grist for Thirkell's mill, and finely did she grind the grain. From the golden summer in which Rose's wedding takes place through the autumn when the storm begins to lower to the spring in which the War finally becomes a horrible monstrous reality instead of a tedium of boring daily life, *Cheerfulness Breaks In* links two eras.

The past world of *The Brandons* is evoked vividly in *Cheerfulness Breaks In*, especially when Mrs. Brandon and her home Stories reappear. Except for the advent of a nursery school with young children and two teachers who are billeted at Stories, the tenor of Mrs. Brandon's life is not greatly changed by the war. The Millers' life is changed much more because they are intimately involved in the day-to-day concerns of the poorer members of the parish and in the billeting and care of the evacuee children. Mrs. Brandon, however, does her embroidery, working on smocks for the evacuee children, and she continues to do the flowers for the church and her home. Her son Francis is still at home, as he is too old to be called up yet for the military, and Delia is doing V. A. D. work at Barchester Infirmary.

That Sir Edmund Pridham should be cruelly troubled by his inability to understand that 1940 is not 1914 is part of the bitter new wartime world (*Cheerfulness Breaks In* 145-47), as is the sermon by Mr. Smith the chaplain at Southbridge School in which he notes that the boys should prepare for the future, even if they don't know what it will hold, especially in light of the spread of totalitarianism (149). Mr. Smith's comments, which pass unremarked as part of the Day of National Prayer, were perhaps more characteristic of the muddled thoughts of most people than the reader might care to think. At the time, of course, Thirkell, like the rest of the citizenry, had no idea of what horrors lay ahead nor of how the life of England was changing, but she was able to pick up the absurdity and pathos of such a sermon and present it for the amusement of her readers. There probably were sermons aplenty delivered which differed very little from her example.

The demands of wartime also meant a mixing of classes which had not before been evident in the world of which Thirkell wrote. The prime example of this mixing in *Cheerfulness Breaks In* is the creation of the Bissells and their home life, and the way in which the Birketts (not to mention Misses Bent and Hampton) and Mrs. Morland find a way through the maze of social difficulties as they come to know each other. In her pre-war novels, Thirkell had illustrated various interactions between the classes in Barsetshire, primarily between the servants, the gentry, and the villagers. But in *Cheerfulness Breaks In*, there are strangers among the natives of Barsetshire. Some are English: the Bissells, the evacuee children, the Warburys.

Others are from further afield, primarily the Mixo-Lydian refugees.

In addition, contemporary history (apart from "a scrap" and The Day of National Prayer) irrupts vividly. The Royal Oak, a British ship which was sunk in the Scapa Flow in the far north of England, was one of the first of many, and it, along with the defeat of the British and French armies at Dunkirk, showed clearly that Thirkell's fictional world was suffering from the destruction of the war and from the terrifying uncertainties of the times (110). It is only in *Cheerfulness Breaks In* that a Thirkell book ends on an unfinished note. Lydia Keith has married Noel Merton and he has been sent abroad just as the marooned British Expeditionary Force is being rescued by the swarms of little boats from the beaches of Dunkirk; Lydia receives a telegram at the end of the book, but the reader is left not knowing whether the wire is to say that Noel has been killed or that he has returned safely (331). This withholding of information illustrates effectively how uncertain the times were. No one knew what the future would hold, of course; looking back on those dark days it is easy to forget that the people who were living through them were anxious and frightened by the uncertainties and dangers with no clear end in sight and no way of knowing Germany would be defeated.

At the end of six years of war, Peace staggered untidily onto the scene, though for Barsetshire as for England, it was not the "golden Peace" which people believed they remembered, but an uncertain, difficult, and gray world where rationing still loomed large, and shortages of all kinds continued to bedevil the exhausted denizens of Britain. *Peace Breaks Out* illuminates this period, and with her usual wit Thirkell shares the mysteries of Barsetshire life, from the curious architecture of Mr. Scatchard's home, Rokeby, in Hatch End, to the remarkable way in which the news of Peace's advent is transmitted by the baker who tells his customers to get all the bread they want tomorrow since there will be none on the following day in celebration of Peace.

In addition, in *Peace Breaks Out* Thirkell returns to elements of the old Barsetshire life. For example, the traditional Sunday morning Anglican service is in full swing, and if there are fewer young men than there had been, there is an absence of the uncertainty and stress of *Cheerfulness Breaks In*. Additionally, the evolving relationships between various young people - Anne Fielding and Robin Dale (he having been invalided out of the Army with an artificial foot), Sylvia Halliday and Martin Leslie (he limping from a serious injury received fighting on the Italian front), and Rose Bingham and David Leslie - take center stage, only slightly impeded by the difficulties of Peace.

Thirkell and her readers slide gently into the post-war world, yet the experiences of the war years have changed a great deal in Barsetshire. The Mixo-Lydians are still very much present. Rationing of food and clothing continues unabated. The Hosiers' Boys' School is, much to the relief of the natives of Southbridge, returning to London, though Mr. Bissell and his wife have come to be a part of the Southbridge world, albeit somewhat despite themselves. In addition, there are the rumours and rumbles of the changes in English society which are beginning to manifest themselves in Barsetshire as they did in the rest of England. Mr. Churchill has had to resign the Government, and the general election is to come, in which the redoubtable Mr.

Sam Adams stands as the Labour candidate for Barsetshire, opposed by Sir Robert Fielding.

Mr. Adams has developed from the overpowering and comic figure of Heather Adams' father in *The Headmistress*. His gradual integration into the world of Barsetshire is one of the themes of the postwar books. Mrs. Morland is expected to come to Southbridge to visit the Birketts, just as she did in *Cheerfulness Breaks In*, though in this case only for the day; Rose Fairweather and her husband appear for a brief visit as well. The characters have grown older and mostly are more tired, but there is hope in Barsetshire, as in England, and the promise of something besides the Brave New (and in Thirkell's view, Revolting) World.

Nonetheless, there is an irrevocable sea-change since the days of *Before Lunch* and *The Brandons*. In these novels of the beginning and the end of the war, the external world is firmly intertwined with Barsetshire, and it will remain so. The political changes and above all the social changes of the post-war years will be interwoven in the tales of Barsetshire; there will be no return to the golden years of *Wild Strawberries,* which seem to exist in a world apart. The often drab and irritating realities of post-war England are illustrated by Thirkell as vividly as are the experiences of the war years. Thirkell's gifts as a writer which include her wit, her exquisite use of the English language and her portraits of her beloved Barsetshire, are matched by her gifts as a social historian.

In both *Cheerfulness Breaks In* and *Peace Breaks Out*, Thirkell segues skillfully from one world to another. In these books, the new stage set is unfolded and put forth, though in both cases it is done with such craftsmanship that the reader doesn't realize that he (or more likely she) is gently being introduced to a new world.

Works Cited

Thirkell, Angela. *Before Lunch*. London: Hamish Hamilton, 1939.

Thirkell, Angela. *The Brandons*. London: Hamish Hamilton, 1939.

Thirkell, Angela. *Cheerfulness Breaks In*. London, Hamish Hamilton, 1940.

Thirkell, Angela. *The Headmistress*. London, Hamish Hamilton, 1944.

Thirkell, Angela. *Peace Breaks Out*. London, Hamish Hamilton, 1946.

Thirkell, Angela. *Wild Strawberries*. London, Hamish Hamilton, 1934

Contributor

Carol Christopher Kelton (Drake) Stone was educated at Radcliffe, the University of Washington, and the University of California at Berkeley, where she earned a B. A. in English and did her honors paper on Angela Thirkell. She since has written extensively on Angela Thirkell and has addressed the Angela Thirkell Society at several national meetings. She has published poetry under the name Carol Christopher Drake, and for the past twenty-eight years she has worked as a pediatric RN in intensive care at Children's Hospital, Oakland, California.

Class Manners, Gossip and War Time Society in Harefield Village: A Domestic History in Angela Thirkell's *The Headmistress*
by
John Childrey

Readers and critics alike will find that it is enlightening to read Angela Thirkell's *The Headmistress* as a social historical narrative, a diary-like account of routine domestic events and ruminations covering roughly a school term in Harefield village in the county of Barsetshire. In particular, the items and events listed and linked into domestic niceties and minor traumas are narrative, not from the perspective of the Hosiers' Girls' Foundation School's Headmistress, but from the perspective of the true "headmistress" of Harefield Park, Lucy Belton. It is Mrs. Belton who is the centering character, but not necessarily the protagonist in the sense that she is the one who has the novel shattering epiphany or the major change; rather, Thirkell has the reader follow Mrs. Belton on her daily duties, so the reader's sense of appropriate manners and ordered society emanates from Mrs. Belton. Thirkell allows the reader access to Mrs. Belton's interior thoughts as well as to her overt actions, and it is in the space between these thoughts and actions that the reader can glimpse domestic order, fear, change and expectation, both personally and publicly, as events unfold.

Thirkell creates and energizes all of her characters with domestic foibles and desires. Three motifs illumine the novel as a historical narrative, and those motifs will help the reader understand the interplay with history as well as with how those motifs impact, augment, or are interspersed with the novel's narrative threads. The three motifs of social status and manners, local and family gossip, and the impact of the war organize the reading. The novel of village life is set subtly against the war outside Harefield, but Mrs. Belton and her compatriots reflect ways that the war and war effort change the social order, social practice, and social manners. The war and war effort also create unexpected circumstances, although the basic fabric of daily life endures.

The thematic elements weave the loss and restoration of the Belton fortunes, the several romantic relationships (real and imagined), the interplay of village life, and the calendar of school events into a humorous, yet often delicate, narrative story fabric, a worsted practical yet warm. The several climatic events seem deft, quick touches, that allow Thirkell to finish the storyline and end the novel. Of course, she leaves enough loose ends to carry over to a next installment. Tea in a fortnight?

Mr. and Mrs. Belton have left their home at Harefield and relocated to Arcot House on the High Street in the village of Harefield because of the war economy, exacerbated perhaps by a hint of fiscal mistakes. The future of Harefield Park appears to be in jeopardy for Freddy Belton, their eldest son. They have let part of the Park to the Hosiers' Girls' Foundation School, and although the family is unhappy that others are in their home, Mrs. Belton bears up well in front of her husband.

The Hosiers' School with its activities and events allows the locals, including the Beltons, to continue some favorite activities from the past, such as ice-skating, and the presence of the school also allows new persons to the village to emerge as important participants in village life. The Headmistress of the school, Miss Sparling, is introduced and accepted into the social fabric of the village, because of her status as headmistress, but just as importantly because of her charming personality. Mr. Carton, the resident intellectual, first accepts her socially and intellectually, partly because of her grandfather's scholarship, but then genuinely because of her own authorship of a scholarly article he much admires. It comes as little surprise that they have "an understanding" by the close of the novel. What might be criticized by the modern reader is the acquiescing nature of Miss Sparling, who chooses directing the school over pursuing her scholarship, instead supporting Carton in his own research on Fluvius Minucius, her original topic.

The reader is admitted to the society of the status class women of Harefield as they involve themselves in the domestic duties of their households, hold working parties in support of the war effort, and deal with family issues. But the reader is also privy to the servant class gossip and chatter, since the servants' stations allow for running commentary and speculation on the families they serve. Additionally, the men of the novel bring their own interpretations of personalities and local issues, from their opinions of the psychological approach of the local woman doctor to their comments on policies and demands of the agricultural council. Tying much of the novel together are the romances or imagined romances of Elsa Belton and Captain Hornby and of Heather Adams and Freddy Belton.

Lucy Belton is the former mistress of Harefield Park, the home for several generations of Beltons. "Mrs. Belton was very tired and blamed herself for the feeling. A woman in her middle fifties, she said angrily to herself, had no business to be tired" (*The Headmistress* 18). She, of course, does have reason to be tired. Her husband has lost Harefield Park, and the Beltons have moved into a tenant house. Her sense of loss is for herself but much more so for her husband, who feels the loss of Harefield Park keenly. Lucy Belton is acutely aware of how disappointed her husband is about the fiscal bind that has forced the leasing of Harefield Park to the girls' school, and yet both the Beltons recognize that the school has helped them out enormously from a financial perspective. Mrs. Belton is especially sensitive to her husband's unstated feeling that, although the Park had been on financial tenterhooks for some time, even dating from the Nabob's extravagances in the late eighteenth century, he is hurt and embarrassed that the loss of the Park had come during his management. She realizes that in spite of his "valiant efforts," the move from the Park represents a loss of status in Barsetshire and in Harefield society for both of them (8). Although her family has not provided any financial assistance in her marriage, Mrs. Belton knows the family name and reputation is excellent but of little practical use in the present straits (8). Although she decries the necessity of the move, she accepts it as well as she can and appreciates the charm of her new home, Arcot House.

This loss of status is a motif that Thirkell uses frequently in *The Headmistress*, tying elements of her narrative to Mrs. Belton's point of view, and it is central to the novel. Thirkell allows the reader to see the events, the world of the village, and her private world view, and she filters the gossip of the village and family, the biases, fears and aspirations, reprimands and disappointments through her honest, if very class conscious, perspective.

Mrs. Belton expresses her anxieties over the imminent arrival of her unmarried children, who are the focus of her aspiration that "the family might at last come into its proper place again," and she dreams simply that Freddy and Elsa will marry well and that Charles will earn a lot of [much needed] money (*The Headmistress* 9). She seems, however, to think that there is little they can do to please their younger son, Charles. There is no question that the Beltons love and fear for their son in the military, but upon hearing his voice in the entryway, they know their well-ordered, quiet existence will be upset for the duration of his visit. To them he seems more immature than do the other children. His tactlessness and self-centeredness both embarrass them and upset their sense of propriety. He demands his independence, yet seems to want a great deal of attention. It seems that Mr. and Mrs. Belton can never do anything just as he wants; Elsa causes similar concerns to a lesser degree, and Freddy is quite mature.

The presentation of Charles Belton in *The Headmistress* is particularly interesting, because in the later books *Love Among the Ruins* and *The Old Bank House*, he is a model of good nature and kindness, guiding Clarissa Graham toward better manners and more sensitivity to others. They become engaged in *The Duke's Daughter* and finally marry in *Happy Return*, with Charles providing the emotional stability she seems to need. In *Enter Sir Robert*, *Never Too Late*, and *Close Quarters*, they end up living back at Harefield Park, where Charles, who is somewhat lacking in ambition and apparently feels no need to repair the family fortunes, is employed as a schoolmaster.

In *The Headmistress*, however, the reader discovers the young Charles' churlish behavior in regard to Heather Adams when she drops her prayer book for him to retrieve (33), and when his mother suggests he dance with Heather (46). Later, he tries to redeem himself when he apologizes for not skating with her, although it is clear enough he has no intention of doing so (267). Charles identifies Heather Adams as one girl he would not want to have occupying his former room at Harefield Park and says so, and he reflects his own class-consciousness in asking Miss Sparling about the class status of the girls at school (48).

Charles's sister Elsa Belton has no end of tactlessness herself as she offers Christopher Hornby's family jewelry for the Red Cross (182) and his money for helping out Harefield Park for her parents (196, 249, 259). Additionally, her outbursts about girls at the Hosiers' School are numerous (33, 127, 142, 196). Even though Elsa refers to herself as a snob, it seems clear that early in the book, she does not understand the manners and tact needed to accompany the responsibilities of birth and social status (34). Captain Hornby admonishes her lovingly and remarks that when they are married, he will probably be promoted, and she will need to behave as an admiral's wife is expected to behave (306).

Freddy Belton to his credit has outgrown whatever childish selfishness or immaturity might cause his mother anxiety, although she worries about his broken heart from his betrothed's death. Freddy is not enamored with Heather Adams, but graciously asks her to dance when his brother slights her (44). Indeed, throughout the book, Freddy's behavior toward Heather Adams reflects his maturity and sense of duty. Freddy also skates with her (266) and rescues her when she falls through the broken ice (268), taking her to Arcot House wrapped in his coat (*The Headmistress* 268-269). Later he sits with Heather Adams, albeit awkwardly realizing her crush on him, and relates the death of his W.R.E.N. love (278). Freddy understands the new wealth that Heather Adams and her father represent, but he responds with an obligation of manners to dispel her girlish fantasy. While he is aware that he will add to her sense of the romantic by sharing his loss, the generosity of his act clearly indicates his social status. But Freddy is, after all, a product of his environment, as he reflects that Harefield Park in its dire financial straits "is practically in the hands of the Jews" (suggesting moneylenders) and jokingly approves of slavery in order to find enough servants (184-85). He also shows respect to his father's concerns over the Park, but interestingly, since Freddy is the eldest son and will inherit, he does not seem to see the future of the Park as his problem to help solve (256-257). Freddy outwardly demonstrates maturity, but like his brother and even his father, he seems to feel no ambition to save the family home or fortune through his own financial initiative or business.

Against the backdrop of these interior tensions the Belton family narrative meanders through fall, winter, and spring in Harefield Village, and through the character of Lucy Belton the reader experiences the social activities and daily sojourn of a family in wartime with adult children in the war effort. Because Lucy Belton provides a centralizing figure, her coping with the family loss of status is of particular interest, as is her class-consciousness. The move from the Park to the High Street, is often co-mingled with daily gossip and the intrusions of the war.

Initially friends fete Mrs. Belton, consoling her for the move from the manor house to the High Street. Lady

Graham sends two rabbits and a basket of mushrooms (*The Headmistress* 10), Lucy Marling brings her grapes and a brace of partridges (13), Lady Pomfret offers shooting privileges to the Belton sons (16), and Lady Norton sends biscuits by a soldier billeting nearby (18). These social niceties, however, come as sympathy for the move from Harefield Park to Arcot House. Even Dr. Perry and Mr. Oriel mention that the entire village will miss the Beltons at the Park (17). It is not surprising that when the entire social circle attempts to ease the apparent loss, they do so through Mrs. Belton, perhaps to allow Mr. Belton to save a shred of dignity, or perhaps they feel an expression of sympathy is the compassionate manner with which to deal with such a public change of status, not just of location. Apparently, however, the details of the lease are not public, for at one point, Mrs. Belton is embarrassed by the suggestion that the Beltons have altruistically provided the Park for the Hosiers' School; she thinks the price of the rent sufficient and wonders if that shouldn't be mentioned also (227).

Elsa flippantly compares Arcot House to a mud hovel, but apparently approves of it with her comment "And how lovely to be home, even if it isn't home. It's a heavenly house, father" (25-26). Elsa's energy and enthusiasm at arriving home propel the scene, which continues topsy-turvy with the arrival of Freddy Belton, as the three children head out to the Nabob, the local pub (named after their ancestor), for a drink before dinner. The occasion allows the reader an early glimpse of the degree of class-consciousness that Lucy Belton exhibits. Copper gives all her children rides from the railroad station, and her first notion is to invite him to join them for an informal dinner, but "Even as she spoke she became aware that the obliging Copper would not be in the least a suitable dinner guest," not with his broken teeth (*The Headmistress* 27). Later she admits to herself that she has much "to be thankful for, [but] life at this particular moment was just too much for her" (28).

After meeting Miss Sparling at church, the Belton family makes her the center of family discussion at lunch in the context of what constitutes a lady. As she is their tenant at the Harefield Park the senior Beltons think their participation in the discussion of the attributes of a lady and whether or not Miss Sparling has them, would be "the height of ill-breeding" (34). Lucy Belton recognizes her own upbringing as sheltered among "her own sort" and she realizes that Elsa is mingling with others who presumably are in positions of importance because of their brains, a meritocracy replacing the social standing of her youth, but she thinks "All this mixing might be a good thing, but she felt too old for it and frankly hated it" (34).

These interior notions are juxtaposed against Mr. Belton's quarrelsome notions about a fellow magistrate who "throws his weight about and gets petrol when nobody else does. . ." (35). This fellow is Sam Adams, a motivated individual and newly wealthy owner of a war plant, and a person who represents the kind of mixing and mingling Lucy Belton hates. Charles makes the analysis that among the men of the tank corps, in the midst of getting dirty and sweaty, he finds that they are "all right," while Mrs. Belton hopes her children will marry "our sort" (35).

Much of the gossip and family discussion concerns this social status and much of the novel deals with trying to adjust to the changes in the social structure that the war effort necessitates. A sense of social class, even to the extent that snobbery plays a part, is a motif of interest.

Again and again Lucy Belton and Elsa bemoan the loss of Harefield Park. As Elsa realizes her change in fortune with Captain Hornby, she wants to use some of his money to support the Red Cross and to preserve the Park for her parents, in a nice sort of balance between serving humanity and serving family. Her manner of persuasion is petulant and bullying, and Captain Hornby blithely ignores her behavior, but also accedes to it as well, albeit in his own manner. He is aware, it seems, of his own social responsibilities to his future in-laws, but those obligations will be accomplished with decorum, and they will be appropriately managed and quietly pursued. This manner of behavior will not only be generous, but also appear genuinely generous to the Beltons and not cause them embarrassment. Such assistance is ultimately not needed, so no one is embarrassed because of the money, except silly Elsa, and Mrs. Belton is able to explain Elsa's bad behavior as part of the engagement jitters (*The Headmistress* 214).

As a reflection of possibly historical importance, Lucy Belton's preoccupation with her own and her family's loss of status in a class conscious Harefield is revealing. It is important to record what the landed gentry and their servants had as concerns, both major and minor. As one might expect, most of the concerns are personal, mundane and comical. Lucy Belton wonders what the tailor would think of her change in status: she feels the tailor might not perform the alterations needed for her clothes as she lost weight, since she was certain he could make more money making new clothes for other customers (73). Mr. Belton comments on a particularly nice sunset and how the views of sunsets from the Park when they lived there were particularly pleasing, but his wife dismisses the notion with what seems an attempt to adapt to her present home (74).

The serving characters are introduced as comic relief, yet they underscore the class-consciousness as well. The interaction between Mr. Oriel's cook, Mrs. Powlett, and his maid, Dorothy, concerning the order in which the lady guests are to be served, as well as other interactions, is as humorous as it is historically instructive, and the tradition of class serving is nicely represented in who has the order of service (*The Headmistress* 75-76). Here in this setting is an understanding that Lucy Belton is given the nod because of her loss of status. Mrs. Powlett makes a complex analysis of the order of importance of the anticipated guests, and concludes that Lucy Belton must be served first because this is her first visit from Arcot House, rather than from the Park (76).

The frequent inter-twining of the Adams family, daughter Heather and father Sam, with that of the Beltons intensifies the apparent loss of status by the Beltons and the rise of the mercantile-industrial segment of society represented by the Adamses. Perhaps the depiction of Heather as an obese, unattractive adolescent with few social graces and a moody personality reflects one perception by a portion of the social gentry. This condescending portrayal seems somewhat ironic in its snobbery since the gentry's skills may be seen as less than useful by a class whose own skills seem highly desirable, practical, and needed in a war effort. Heather's adolescent attempts at flirting may be a thinly disguised analogy of the desire of the industrial class for gentry class recognition. When Heather drops her prayer book to attract Charles Belton, she wants to be accepted and noticed by the handsome and attractive gentleman (33). Charles ignores her attempts, but Freddy's manners prevail. Practical considerations and merit necessitate the mixing of classes. Whether or not this class flirtation is conscious or simply part of the social fabric of the times, Thirkell pointedly weaves the Adamses' story against and into the Beltons' story with its reversal of fortune.

Heather and her father provide items of gossip, and the progression of comments chronicles not only class and personal distinction, but also highlights, in Heather's storyline, both attractive and unattractive characteristics. She is easily dismissed as a dour and clumsy girl with few friends and fewer redeeming qualities. She attempts to have Charles notice her, but is rebuffed or ignored (*The Headmistress* 34, 46). To balance adverse commentary on her appearance, Miss Sparling singles out Heather's excellence in the study of mathematics (46). Her size, appearance, and appetite come in for much commentary (49, 95-96, 1195, 218), as even the cook points out that Heather seems to be eating for two (49, 95-96, 195, 218). Thirkell has fun with this remark, which otherwise generally indicates pregnancy, having Mrs. Powlett tell the Hosiers' school cook, who has an illegitimate child, "It's not for you to talk about eating for two. You've done that once too often" (218).

Mr. Belton finds that Heather is not afraid of rats and thinks this a highly prized characteristic in a girl (13), and Heather is also an able skater, willingly accepting the responsibility of helping the younger girls in their skating (254-255). Her growing maturity is reflected in the change from her romantic desire to join the W.R.E.N.s and be a heroine (117), to an acceptance that she could put her mathematical gifts to better use in her father's industrial war plant at Hogglestock (287). Heather's change of choices probably reflects societal changes as well: as the war progresses, more choices are accepted as aiding the war effort. Thematically, Heather's choice of assisting the industrial aspect of the war effort parallels the presumed military deployment of Charles, Freddy and Captain (soon to be Admiral) Hornby.

Sam Adams is presented as a large man; physically powerful and large in importance, his size assists his acceptance into the society of the shire. Unlike his daughter, he is neither dour nor retiring. He owns the Hogglestock Rolling Mills and sits with Mr. Belton on the Barsetshire magisterial bench. Mr. Updike, the lawyer/ solicitor, provides the information that Sam Adams has no background, but that he has been made a member of the county club (*The Headmistress* 158), and Mr. Carton, recognizing Adams' ascendancy, wryly calls him "One of our Conquerors" (158). Apparently, while Adams irritates Mr. Belton with his behavior concerning some court issues, Mr. Belton recognizes that Mr. Adams has a skill for recognizing and understanding the business side of government and its call for contracts. Mr. Adams is very skillful in obtaining governmental contracts and in providing for those in need (158). Lucy Belton defends Mr. Adams, sight unseen, to Mr. Carton (158), but when she sees Mr. Adams at Bobbin Day at the Hosiers' School, she is put off by the over-hairiness of the backs of his hands and the forwardness of his self-introduction (225, 234).

Mr. Belton seems so absorbed in his own events that he initially patronizes Sam Adams, but Mr. Adams sympathizes with and ultimately assists Mr. Belton against the plans of the agricultural council for Church Meadow (176-1777, 300-301). As a result, Mr. Belton indicates that he had recognized Sam Adams as a "good fellow" from the start, but Mrs. Belton calls him on that piece of misinformation and re-interpretation of fact (300). Mr. Adams' usefulness and clout with war boards reflects the recognition, even grudgingly given, of practical and leveraged action, and Sam Adams is the first major character to cross societal lines for practical reasons.

Miss Sparling, the Hosiers' School's Headmistress, is accepted into Harefield society because of her pleasant and agreeable personality (*The Headmistress* 4, 80), and she is accepted into Mr. Carton's academic society/class when he finds that she has authored a scholarly paper in the tradition of her grandfather, Canon Horbury (164-165). Finally, she is accepted into the Hosier Company based upon her merit and service to the school under very trying circumstances after the school was destroyed in the bombing of London (229). Miss Sparling reflects a separate means for crossing lines of class, gender and society in a traditionally class-conscious milieu.

The Belton family status is based not upon merit but upon the ancestral "Nabob," the family nickname for the forebear who made his money in the East India Trade, purchasing the lands of Harefield Park upon the misfortunes of the previous owners (3). The Nabob achieved for his family a rise in status from a trading class to landed gentry. So there is an underlying falseness in the Beltons' class-consciousness, but Lucy Belton changes as much or more than anyone in this narrative, offering a balance between class snobbishness and excellent manners. She achieves her status not only by marrying into the Belton family, but also through her Thorne relatives, whose bloodlines are good though somewhat undistinguished. Lucy Belton provides the prism through which the reader sees the nuances and subtleties of this class mixing: Lucy Belton does not approve, but she is one of the means through which change is effected.

A list of war references suggests the kinds of items and events that reflect the historical context of the period of the narrative, and Thirkell shows how the world events that swirl around Harefield impact lives in small, but significant ways. Elsa Belton during her leave discusses the prospects for marriage, especially in light of the economic downturn of the family and notes that eligible young men die in the war (*The Headmistress* 35). Mrs. Hoare complains that if her daughter lived in England instead of Australia, Mrs. Hoare would probably be left with all of her four grandchildren, which would be an impossible responsibility without household help (58). Mrs. Updike loathes the holidays as there is no leave for her children, and the holidays cause her to fear that the war will continue long enough to involve the younger children (146). Heather Adams fantasizes over Freddy Belton's imagined war wound (205), and Freddy reveals the death of his love interest/ W.R.E.N. fiancée to his mother (186) and to Heather in what Thirkell refers to as "a most heroic deed" (279). Finally, Lucy Belton remembers Porthos' death from the *The Three Musketeers* as she muses on the possibility of Charles' death when she sees his clothes in disarray (289).

Food and food rationing have an integral role in daily life as the war motif plays itself out in various discussions and events. Thirkell infuses the narrative with many examples of food shortages that reflect the domestic changes occasioned by the war. By this point in the war years, the meat and cheese were at a "minimum" and fish was rarely available, but Thirkell adds the highly perceptive detail that what fish there were, were in a "distinctly tired condition" (153). Almost all foodstuffs were either restricted, rationed, or not available, so many people who wish to entertain are reduced to serving only tea, and the village women even need to bring their own milk for tea during their working party (*The Headmistress* 55-57). This necessity allows Thirkell to reflect on persons who conveniently forget or who are selfishly absent-minded in not providing their own portions, thus infringing on the rationing portion of the hostess or the other women. Some discussion of powdered milk ensues as well, and at least two discussions of the use of saccharine prompt mention of its use instead of sugar as part of the war effort. (65, 66, 11, 67-68) For the villagers this substitution of sugar is a domestic inconvenience but Thirkell does not mention the part it plays in the manufacture of gunpowder, a connection which probably seemed self-evident in 1943.

Home-grown vegetables and meat, as well as game, are available as un-rationed food, so individuals resort to maintaining home gardens and chicken houses (97). The issue of the care and cleaning of chickens by Lucy Belton is occasioned by Mrs. Updike's offer of one of her young cockerels (97-100), partridges are discussed (132), and comments appear again on the freshness and availability of fish (78). Lucy Belton arranges with the butcher for meat when she knows her children will be home. She wants something "off the ration" for them, so the butcher includes three chops and a kidney "for the cat" (245).

Other rationing incidents include gas (petrol) rationing that limit travel, so the Hosiers' schoolgirls are reduced to shared transportation during their trips home for the holidays (144). Sam Adams feels he needs to justify his travel to Bobbin Day and to the Beltons as necessary war related travel when he visits Heather (240, 282). Rationed stamps are limited to four envelopes per day (98), and letters are posted with economy labels (250). Other commodities in limited supply are coal for heating (221-

222) and binding for books (*The Headmistress* 210). During a working party, several of the women discuss work-worn hands, the lack of ointment for such (64), and the lack of servants (64-65). Mrs. Perry feels the need to justify her continued use of a maid who is luckily above the "calling up age" (65). Even Freddy knows that silk is in short supply and in rather tongue-in-cheek manner suggests that Elsa use a white tablecloth for her wedding dress (185-186).

On other issues, the War Agricultural Executive Committee requests that Mr. Belton plough under Church Meadow for agricultural purposes (37, 176-177). Security and safety clash as the villagers move from house to house after dark; Mrs. Hoare mentions blackout curtains (173); Florrie leaves the Beltons' light on in Charles' room after setting the blackout curtains (289); and flashlights or torches provide consternation when used in the dark (104).

Political issues are raised several times, with Mrs. Perry and Mrs. Hunter providing the point-counter-point. The Mixo-Lydians and the Slavo-Lydians represent the inner-war among the village women of the narrative (50, 68-69, 71, 86-87). Mrs. Perry espouses one side (157, 172-173) and even brings the Brownscus to Bobbin Day activities (236). Mrs. Hunter talks about a particular Slavo-Lydian (236), and Sam Adams completes the story as the Slavo-Lydian had attempted to advocate a worker vs. management socialistic program among the Hogglestock workers (237). Not only political, this internal taking sides reflects the nature of the war, providing some discussion of the presumed merits, faults, and character of the combatants, both in the conflict and the narrative. The connection with other of Thirkell's novels provides a historical fantasy for someone to chronicle the Mixo- and

Slavo-Lydian conflict and perhaps draw the appropriate parallels to the history of the Balkans.

Some individual attitudes emerge almost in passing that reflect various other irritants caused by the war and war effort. Mr. Belton prefers that Harefield Park be used as a school rather than for billeting forces, since he fears they may burn it down (*The Headmistress* 52), but "billet" is the term Miss Sparling uses referring to the time the Hosier girls spent at Barsetshire High after bombing destroyed their school in London (200). Dr. Perry suggests that married women are exercising their libidos with soldiers while their husbands are absent (16), and the Russians are reported to be trying to reunify the churches by installing a Patriarch (87). Finally, Mrs. Hoare in her enthusiasm for Shakespeare believes that the difficulties of the war allow his plays to call for all persons and castes to "pull together" (172).

The war and war effort provide other opportunities for Thirkell to weave a domestic tapestry. Another part of the narrative is the framework of the school and school year activities, the outings into the Park, the Bobbin Day activities and theatricals, and the skating party. The episodes involving the characters and characteristics of the girls and schoolmistresses provide additional points of comparison for schools and for exploring how they carried on during the war years.

Frank Kermode argues that "acts of interpretation are required [to understand narrative] at every stage in the life of a narrative … Secular authors also interpret their own fables…." (ix). Thirkell certainly creates her Harefield fable in a manner that easily disguises it as the narrative gossip of neighbors. She concentrates in the interior comments of Lucy Belton primarily, but liberally fills in others' notions and interior feelings as well, most noticeably those of Madeleine Sparling. Because Thirkell uses this device in her domestic historical narrative, the title of the novel, *The Headmistress*, carries the appropriately ambiguous weight of being a novel of both of these women. They do not compete in a traditional way, but rather serve to reflect at least two aspects of society and to expedite the inevitable change in a class-conscious world that is exemplified by the rise of the industrialist, Sam Adams, even more directly. Miss Sparling's accomplishments and her well-bred demeanor elevate her in the village society early in the narrative and nothing that happens diminishes that elevated position.

The actions and events, mundane and dramatic, happen as ordinarily as breathing. Kermode characterizes such a narrative sense: "The world to the outsider is obscurely organized and it's a blessing, though possibly a delusive one, that the world is also ... 'patient of interpretation' in terms of whatever happens to interest us" (ix). One of the "blessings" for the reader of 1943 would have been the sense of the orderly chaos Thirkell presents of the home front. There is a sense of security and calmness in the gossip and in the comings and goings of the women's work parties knitting for the Barsetshire boys, a kind of universal statement that every segment of society is sharing in the privations, but these same mothers and sisters, brothers and uncles, are also dealing with similar frustrations involved in the secret movements, rationing, censorships, irrational bureaucratic pronouncements and policies, and the like. The novel is rife with reminders that mothers have fears for the safety of sons, the security of daughters, and the well being of husbands.

Moreover, the Lucy Beltons and their Wheelers would have been very familiar to her readers, the latter name likely causing a chuckle with the currency of the concept 'wheeler-dealer' being discovered or re-discovered in a new generation, being able to procure cockerels, fresh fish, a extra portion of chops, or seemingly what was needed. These staples, not just of narrative characters, but also of real mothers, nurses, housekeepers, school headmistresses, neighbors, must have brought images of home and hearth to those separated from home. Thirkell's is a domestic history that aids the war effort, raises morale, and elicits a laugh or tear in the events, both very real and very slight, portrayed.

In discussing the secrecy of narrative, Kermode makes an important observation that seems appropriate for novels and especially for Thirkell's domestic narrative:

> Insiders read and perceive, but always in a different sense ... And we interpret always as transients ... both in the book and in the world which resembles the book. For the world is our beloved codex. [As readers] we can travel back and forth at will, divining congruences, conjunctions, opposites; extracting secrets from its secrecy, making understood relations, an appropriate algebra. This is the way we satisfy ourselves with explanations of the unfollowable world – as if it were a structured narrative, of which more might always be said by trained readers, by insiders. (144-145)

Many of Thirkell's 1943 readers were "insiders" who were able to put real, remembered, faces to the characters she created. Hundreds of High Streets of villages like Harefield, pubs, solicitors' offices, and schools emerging where manor houses had been were real triggers to memory. The childhood fantasies, romantic crushes, interference of bullies, emergence of ugly ducklings (girl or boy) were their story, or so close to their story that it is little wonder that *The Headmistress* is among the most popular of Thirkell's novels. Its characters, themes, gossip, loves, war efforts, and intrusions resonate of those times and resonate with the current time of global tensions.

There are influences and linkages between parts of society, the family, and the village, and among classes of individuals and groups that invariably clash and accommodate. "Throughout history political and economic events reverberated in the domestic sphere, revising and redefining the norms and structures [of society]" (Weisgrau). In Angela Thirkell's *The Headmistress*, readers find a domestic narrative set in a historically accurate context. The events both worldwide and limited to Barsetshire revise and redefine the Beltons, the Adamses, the Hosiers' Girls' Foundation School, Harefield Park, and reverberate among the other characters as each deals with his or her own issues, with the all-encompassing war effort, and with changes in society.

Works Cited

Kermode, Frank. *The Genesis of Secrecy: On the Interpretation of Narrative* [Charles Eliot Norton Lectures]. Cambridge, Massachusetts: Harvard University Press, 1979.

Thirkell, Angela. *Close Quarters*. London: Hamish Hamilton, 1958.

Thirkell, Angela. *The Duke's Daughter*. London: Hamish Hamilton, 1951.

Thirkell, Angela. *Enter Sir Robert*. London: Hamish Hamilton, 1955.

Thirkell, Angela. *The Headmistress*. New York: Alfred A. Knopf, Inc., 1945 [orig. 1944].

Thirkell, Angela. *Love Among the Ruins*. London: Hamish Hamilton, 1948.

Thirkell, Angela. *Never Too Late*. London: Hamish Hamilton, 1956.

Thirkell, Angela. *The Old Bank House*. London, Hamish Hamilton, 1949.

Weisgrau, Maxine "Family Historically and Cross-Culturally." Special Topics Course Description. Barnard College www.barnard.edu/fysem/specialtopicsF04.html , Fall 2004.

Contributor

John Childrey earned his doctorate from the University of Virginia and his Master of Fine Arts degree from Florida International University. His publications include two books of poetry, *Shadow Words* and *Paradise: An Anthology of Poetry and Prose*, in addition to other poems, and articles on literacy, linguistics, and pedagogy. Nineteen of his poems were collected as "Echoes of the Buffalo Grass" in *Nomad and Standby: A Journal of Custeriana and Amerindiana*. He is currently writing an historical novel based on his research about the 1869-73 voyage of the *U. S. S. Terror*. He is a Professor of English and a former Associate Dean at Florida Atlantic University, where he teaches courses in Metaphor as Interdisciplinary Study, Southern Literature, Adolescent Literature, Grammar, and Creative Writing. He is currently working on an intensive index for *The Headmistress* and on an in-depth study of Heather Adams.

Home in Barsetshire
by
Jay Strafford

On a dreary Saturday afternoon in the late autumn of 1974, I was going home, not to my small city apartment, but home. I had left Richmond, where I was a young newspaper reporter, and had driven about 100 miles west through Piedmont Virginia to mountainous Nelson County, where my ancestors had settled the Rockfish Valley. My widowed mother was living with her widowed mother at the home place, the Fork Farm (the north and south forks of the Rockfish River meet within its acreage). As I crested the hill at Greenfield, I could see Pine Hill, behind which lay the farm. As I began the descent, my car radio was playing the chorus to John Denver's "Back Home Again": "Hey, it's good to be back home again. Sometimes, this old farm feels like a long-lost friend."

The farm was certainly a longtime friend. It was part of a large tract acquired originally by my great-great grandfather, and my grandmother had inherited it from her aunt. On it, my grandparents raised cattle and corn - as well as two daughters, one of them my mother, who married in 1948. Although my family moved to Ohio in 1956, my mom, my younger brother and I spent every summer for many years with my grandparents on the farm, and I stayed there the summer after I graduated from high school, when my grandfather's health was failing.

When I received my degree in journalism from Ohio University in 1973, I couldn't wait to return to Virginia. When my mother was widowed three months later, she and my younger brother moved to the farm, which had always been home in the spiritual sense and now was home in the literal one, as well. All of which struck me with sweet force that November day as I was approaching the farm. How right the singer/songwriter had it. Home is indeed a friend, long lost or always nearby.

* * *

The sense of home accounts for a major appeal of Angela Thirkell's Barsetshire novels. In them, with skill and affection, Thirkell creates a real world, one that feels safe, one that exudes love - but also one in which loss is no stranger.

In physical terms, home means a place - an edifice of some sort. In constructing Barsetshire, Thirkell built a number of homes. From the stately (Pomfret Towers, Rushwater House, Marling Hall, Brandon Abbey, Rising Castle) to the more modest (Jutland Cottage, the cozy vicarages, the Red House at Marling), Thirkell indelibly imparts images of rural England.

But home means people, as well. And Thirkell's skill in character creation rivals that of her literary ancestor, Anthony Trollope, whose novels Nathaniel Hawthorne called: "just as real as if some giant had hewn a great lump out of the earth and put it under a glass case, with all its inhabitants going about their daily business and not suspecting that they were being made a show of" (Letter).

Through her deft characterizations, Thirkell creates a host of people her readers feel they know, people who remind those readers of real-life kinfolk and neighbors. Among her most memorable are:

- Lady Emily Leslie, a blithe spirit, a model of benevolence. If progressively scatterbrained as she grows older, she nonetheless makes herself beloved to all, and her death in *The Old Bank House* closes an era in Barsetshire.
- Laura Morland, Thirkell's apparent self-portrait, a woman of more skills and life knowledge than she gives herself credit for.
- Sam Adams, the self-made man who allows his climb to fortune to erase neither his humanity, nor his sense of duty.
- Maude Bunting, the gentle but firm governess most readers would have liked to have had for a grade-school teacher.
- Dorothea Merriman, secretary and companion and quiet arranger of life for so many, the kind of person who, as Eleanor Roosevelt said of her secretary Malvina "Tommy" Thompson, "makes life possible for me" (Goodwin 27).

The list could go on, and on, and on. But these are five examples of Thirkell's pillars, people without whom communities would function much less well and homes would be much less inviting.

No home, of course, is wholly pleasant, and neither is Barsetshire. Thirkell also creates a number of, if not villains, at least characters who remind her readers of people they try to avoid. Among them are:

- Joyce Smith, the meddlesome landlady who, despite renting the Red House furnished to the Harveys, keeps returning to reclaim items she cannot live without.
- Mrs. Major Spender, the kind of person who never draws a breath without speaking, who thinks silence is an abomination, and who drives to distraction anyone unfortunate enough to be in the same room with her.
- Geoffrey and Frances Harvey, the siblings so obnoxious that the reader feels less sympathy for them than might otherwise have been possible, given Mrs. Smith's constant intrusions.
- Sir Ogilvy Hibberd, later Lord Aberfordbury, the type of do-gooder who is certain he always knows what is best for everyone.
- Francis Brandon and David Leslie, both charming, but both, as his father says often of David, "bone selfish."

Like the list of the pleasant, the list of the annoying also could go on and on. But as the Barsetshire novels never dwell on the unpleasant, neither should the reader.

Although people, of course, are the primary focus, Thirkell populates Barsetshire with some memorable four-legged denizens, as well. The antics of and references to animal characters such as Holdings Goliath and Pompey (what a great name for a hog!) and the various Rushwater bulls come as even more comic relief in essentially comic works.

No home, naturally, would be worth the meaning of the word without love, and Thirkell makes the most of the subject, pairing off lovers - sometimes in surprising couplings - in every book except *Enter Sir Robert*. To the delight of the middle-aged and older, she does not waste love only on the young. Pairings such as Miss Merriman and the Rev. Herbert Choyce, and Mrs. Brandon and Bishop Joram, prove that love truly is for all ages. Particularly satisfying is middle-aged spinster Margot Phelps (and who among us has never known such a woman who sacrifices her independence to care for her aging parents?) eventually finding love with not one, but two men: the vegetable magnate Donald Macfadyen and, when he dies, the beloved pastor Tubby Fewling. Neither - to her credit, and particularly in her era -does Thirkell ignore the differently oriented, such as, apparently, Miss Hampton and Miss Bent.

Thirkell's focus is on the ordinary lives of ordinary people in small towns and rural areas; such lives are particularly vivid to those who hail from such little spots of paradise. But even those who come from, and remain in, the concrete canyons of the world can relate to the people of Barsetshire - human nature is human nature, wherever it dwells. For example, the spirit of the country clergymen whom Thirkell depicts so well, for instance, also lives in the magnificent cathedrals (although perhaps not in some bishops' palaces!).

As in all homes, those in Barsetshire experience the full circle of life, from birth to death. In Barsetshire, death comes generally at the end of the day, not in the middle. Thirkell writes touchingly of death, whether that of Miss Bunting or, as in *The Old Bank House*, of Lady Emily Leslie:

They sat in silence for a while and then Martin said he must go. "Wait one moment," said Lady Emily, holding his hand in her own. "I am coming."

A pang went through Martin's heart as he felt the slight, frail bones in his grandmother's hand, and he waited quietly.

"You have walked so far and so fast," said Lady Emily, with a ghost of her old mischievous smile, "but here I am at last, my darling."

Martin remained perfectly still. There was no sound but the soft warm rain outside the window. Then he laid his grandmother's hand very gently upon her shawl and got up, painfully, and taking his stick went to find Miss Merriman. (313)

* * *

My grandmother, like Lady Emily the gentle strength of her family, died in 1977, and the family sold the Fork Farm a year later. I still drive by it occasionally - never turning in, of course - and still consider it, in a very real sense, home. In my mind's eye, I can see every room at the Fork Farm as it was, and so can I see every home, every village, every inhabitant of Barsetshire. And though I cannot (or will not) make the turn into that long Virginia driveway, I can always open a Barsetshire novel and find home - comfort and familiarity, family and friends - on every page.

Works Cited

Denver, John. *Back Home Again.* 1974. retrieved from
www.lyricsfreak.com, January 2005.

Goodwin, Doris Kearns. *No Ordinary Time.* New York: Simon &
Schuster, 1974.

Hawthorne, Nathaniel. Letter to James Fields. 11 February 1860.
retrieved from www.trollopesociety.org, January 2005.

Thirkell, Angela. *Enter Sir Robert.* London: Hamish Hamilton, 1955.

Thirkell, Angela. *The Old Bank House.* London: Hamish Hamilton,
1949.

Contributor

Jay Strafford holds a journalism degree from Ohio University and has
worked for *The Athens* (Ohio) *Messenger, The* (Cleveland) *Plain
Dealer,* and *The Richmond News Leader.* He has been a reporter, line
editor, copy editor, and page designer. He reads mysteries,
biographies, and British fiction and nonfiction, and is also a published
poet. He is currently with *The Richmond Times-Dispatch,* where he is a
frequent book reviewer when he is not reading Angela Thirkell, whom
he discovered in 1995 with *Marling Hall* from *A Common Reader*
catalogue.

Love Among the Ruins:
Interpreting England in Lady
Emily Leslie
by
Mary Faraci

Angela Thirkell takes on the delightful task in *Love Among the Ruins* of arranging for the birthday party of Lady Emily Leslie. Readers, too, are invited to participate in the preparations to honor this very English subject's life. Resonating like all birthday celebrations, this one's preparations draw readers to look into Lady Emily's eyes, which seem to know more than they can teach about living in the England of poets. Lady Emily's daughter Agnes has faith that her mother, resting during a break in the party, is writing poetry (*Love Among the Ruins* 309). Readers learn later that Lady Emily had imagined a reading at the birthday service that would include extracts from her own vast collection of various literary quotes (356).

Entering her plots as an interested participant, supervising lovingly the details of the grand event, the aging Lady Emily [Laura Collins writes "nearly eighty" years old (46)] gains permission to attend her birthday party from Dr. Ford, who is "all for old people killing themselves in their own way," and points out that Lady Emily is "more likely to kill her family by her vitality than [to kill] herself" (302). The birthday party event returns the characters again and again, in the midst of eating and visiting, to search Lady Emily's eyes for knowledge (316-17).

Thirkell stages the event as if for the joy of drawing from the warmest "thank you" speeches in English literary history as Lady Emily says three times, "Thank you all," and the third utterance resonates as if England herself were speaking: "Thank you all, from my heart, and may Rushwater have new children and new love and new life from generation to generation. God bless you all" (*Love Among the Ruins* 319-322). Thirkell then restores to Lady Emily her usual wide-ranging mind and attention to detail, two of several layers of character that have captured the imagination of readers of the Barsetshire novels. Thirkell writes that immediately following the very gracious and dignified blessings, Lady Emily searches for her spectacles, a typical juxtaposition of the sublime with the ridiculous (322).

Following another reference to Lady Emily's eyes in *Love Among the Ruins* (152), readers discover Thirkell's genius in rereading her character Lady Emily as a loving subject of an England known for its history represented and interpreted in poetry handed down through the ages.

The book-length study by Penelope Fritzer, *Ethnicity and Gender in the Barsetshire Novels of Angela Thirkell*, has done much to create interest in the academy for Thirkell, and Fritzer notes that "Thirkell has been compared to Jane Austen, but she is Shakespearean in her knowledge of human nature" (104). In light of Fritzer's appreciation of the Shakespearean Thirkell, readers are reminded of Thirkell's consciousness that her pen is always moving across a great English literary tradition of representing effects of English wars on English fields, English cathedral cities, English great houses, and English great families.

In the essay "Racial Memory and Literary History," Stephen Greenblatt reminds readers of the novels of Jane Austen, with whom Thirkell is often compared, that Austen draws attention to the English as subjects who "possess Shakespeare as a common bond, a supremely powerful expression of what is shared across all the potentially damaging divisions of class, caste, and interest, a symbol of what is most precious to the nation as a whole" (Greenblatt 51).

Thirkell's English returns again and again to the literary foundations created in Shakespeare's poetry. One wonders, for example, if Thirkell created the wonderful Jessica Dean for the opportunity to remind readers of the nation's common bond: in one particularly humorous passage, Oliver Marling suggests that he could make a witty and apropos remark if Jessica only knew her Shakespeare and so could recognize the remark, and she trumps him by quoting the appropriate passage, at which he apologizes and asks her when she will act in Shakespeare, since she knows him so well (*Love Among the Ruins* 86). With typical Thirkell humor, Jessica replies, mocking the tradition of well-established, middle-aged, actresses playing young ingénues: "When I am about forty-five and ripe for Rosalind" (86).

Later, Thirkell enables the reader to see Lady Emily in a Shakespearean setting: Lucy Marling moves through Lady Emily's room, with all its artifacts, which Thirkell compares to the crowded apothecary's shop from *Romeo and Juliet* (122). More than merely constitutive of cultural literacy, the "Englishness" effects of Shakespeare's plays on the shire are real. Thirkell makes Lady Emily's room the setting for the glorious history of England's leaders recorded in Shakespeare's plays, for crowded among the objects are many signed portraits of England's famous political leaders (*Love Among the Ruins* 122).

The literary representation of an England known through Shakespeare's English is kept alive in Thirkell's successful experiments in portraying the world in which Lady Emily lives. Like Lady Emily's room and like the apothecary shop, post-World War II England is a little world, "at an alarming tilt," however, since among the objects observed in the room is a mirror that shows a skewed view of the world (122). Like Lady Emily, post-World War II England was showing signs of "a gradual coming of old age and ... not in the least an invalid or going mad" (160). Like Lady Emily, post-World War II England captured the effects of a glorious past in the signs of beauty and grace in the present moment: despite their increased weaknesses and confusion, both England and Lady Emily are still beautiful, still beacons of love and kindness (124).

Thirkell chooses to mix poetic images of Lady Emily's face and eyes familiar to readers of the series with classic poetic images of light and lamp to honor this English subject's life while she is still alive. Honoring precious memories of a grand history, Lady Emily's niece, Lady Pomfret, remarks that she wants her aunt to identify photographs in an album, especially the unlabelled royals (161). Managing to restore other layers of meaning to Lady Emily's [and England's] character, Thirkell expresses Lady Pomfret's concern, having her ask Lucy Marling for reassurance that Lady Emily is not really ill (161).

Summarizing the effects achieved in Thirkell's writing, Fritzer finds, "The novels are . . . nationalist . . . yet they are also kindly, witty, and sharp" (4). Discovering the several effects of Thirkell's writing means acknowledging that the writer is always rewriting herself into the plot as various English subjects of Barsetshire. Thirkell seems to have enjoyed discovering again and again in the English language she knew better than anyone, the relationship of the writer to the process of writing. Fritzer, for example, notes that "Thirkell is willing to allow for the wide-ranging play of her own mind in the midst of various events and plots" (103). Continuing to point to passages where Thirkell puts herself inside the creative process, Fritzer concludes: "Thirkell is, then, very honest with her readers by allowing them to see the creative process" (104). Defending the novels about and after World War II against criticism of Thirkell as a too-strong and arrogant commentator, Fritzer places Thirkell among the loving, lamenting, and great writers of wars, fields, cities, and families represented in English literary history: "Thirkell laments a lost world, but they are stronger novels for their increased comments on social history" (5). Inviting readers inside the creative process, Thirkell creates a place for Barsetshire in English literary history: "[T]he immediate postwar novels are much the richer for the sharp social commentary of the brave new world of the Labor government and the myriad changes in England after World War II . . .. [N]ovels focusing on the contemporary social scene are immeasurably stronger for including both events and views of that scene" (Fritzer 5-6).

To understand how Thirkell creates the wonderful effects as she narrates English "social history," one can turn to French linguistic and literary theory. A lost grammatical category marked by endings in ancient languages is the *middle voice* in which the subject is the agent as in the active voice and is also the affected participant as in the passive voice: "In the active, the verbs denote a process that is accomplished outside the subject. In the middle [...]

the verb indicates a process centering in the subject, the subject being inside the process" (Benveniste 148). In today's English, for example, the verb *reads* as in "This book reads well" is the "uncommon voice" neither active nor passive (Barry 141). The French literary critic looked to the ancient category as a way to describe any modern writer's relationship to the creative process (Barthes 143). Thirkell achieves the wonderful effects acknowledged by her most devoted readers by restoring to her English the lost category—not by marking verbs and subjects with ancient inflections, but by imagining herself as a middle voice subject. Thirkell is always inside the process of narrating social history: "One cannot explain these things. One aristocracy, one landed caste, gradually perishes. Another gradually takes its place and in its own time will decay in the eternal cycle of change" (*Love Among the Ruins* 377). The reflection, from the first page of chapter eleven, serves to remind the reader that the author is always wondering aloud about "these things."

Lady Emily's "thank you" remarks above also put faith in "new children and new love and new life from generation to generation" (322). Thirkell avoids an arrogant reporting style; rather, she lets the English language teach her and her readers something new about grand themes like the eternal cycle of change, as well as about purely silly elements of the language itself. Among the more playful linguistics displays in *Love Among the Ruins*, for example, is Thirkell's test of the reader's expectations for the object of "ran over" when the subject is "car": "As Susan drove into Barchester in her little car, she *ran over the names of eligible gentlemen* in her mind" [italics mine] (76). It is Thirkell's pleasure to enter the English language as one of its subjects.

In his work, *The Country and the City,* Raymond Williams is disappointed in Trollope's "ease with schemes of inheritance" (174) and merely "pastoral trimmings" (175) in the Barsetshire novels. He could find in Thirkell's Barsetshire what is missing from Trollope's novels: that "searching analysis" in "a real social history" of "rural England" (Williams 174). Readers find in Lady Emily Leslie a complex image of English life in the busy shifting relations in the shire. Robert Browning imagines the ruins of a city in his poem, "Love among the Ruins." The painting, *Love Among the Ruins*, by Thirkell's grandfather, Sir Edward Burne-Jones, imagines the ruins of great columns. At once a muse to inspire Thirkell and a force to inspire the shire, Lady Emily gives an English flavor to Greek and Roman pastoral themes.

Published in 1947, *Love Among the Ruins* produces one-of-a-kind effects in its interpretation of the contemporary social scene through Thirkell's creation of Lady Emily Leslie. Capturing Thirkell's wit and warmth, Laura Collins draws attention to the care with which Thirkell presents Lady Emily in her appearances throughout the series (43-49). Drawn as "maddening but amusing" (Collins 43) or "far more annoying than charming" throughout the series (Fritzer 69), Lady Emily seems to have been specifically prepared by Thirkell to speak for England in *Love Among the Ruins* as a devoted English subject. While Lady Emily celebrates a birthday with family in *Love Among the Ruins*, Thirkell waits until the next novel in the series, *The Old Bank House*, to write the death scene. The special literary effects of the world in the mind of Lady Emily serve to make readers see familiar literary images and hear familiar speeches known to represent the everyday world of England as Thirkell recreates them. Indebted to a great literary tradition, Thirkell recalls images—as fragments sometimes in Lady Emily's speeches—of loved ones, great speeches, and grand houses.

It is in the figure of Lady Emily that Thirkell finds a muse to celebrate English history. Each appearance makes room for the face of England: the birthday party in *Love Among the Ruins* draws attention to past celebrations and loved ones gone. With a unique mind of her own, Lady Emily knows more about Englishness than she can teach either to the other characters or to the reader. In building the event of the birthday party around Lady Emily, Thirkell reaches readers who experience disturbance even in her Barsetshire. Accounting for the popular reception of noncanonical works by American writers from 1790 to 1860, Jane Tompkins employs the phrase "cultural work of American fiction" (Tompkins ix)—a useful phrase for appreciating what Thirkell does in English fiction: first, creating lively narrative effects in each description of Lady Emily, and, second, recollecting images of complex lives in a shire created out of the history of the development of English land and the development of English cathedral cities.

Breaking out of a pastoral picture of England, Barsetshire's Lady Emily speaks for the England that will not be fixed on a page: wars and age have altered her sense of place. Thirkell recounts the uneasy struggle of Lady Emily's moves from house to house. On every page, the reader is invited to reread the literary and social history of England: the school, the poetry, the cathedral, the couples, and the ruins are all very English. Thirkell knows how to make the reader understand Lady Emily's moral force as a reminder of Englishness.

J.R.R. Tolkien's biographer, Humphrey Carpenter, records as a force at work in Tolkien's writing, "his desire to create a mythology for England," and quotes Tolkien's words: "I had a mind to make a body of more or less connected legend . . . which I could dedicate simply: to England; to my country" (Carpenter 89-90). Impressed with Tolkien's words, "a mythology for England," Professor Jane Chance published in 1979, and recently revised, her book of criticism *Tolkien's Art: 'A Mythology for England.'* Tolkien currently is receiving renewed scholarly attention as a writer dedicated to giving Englishness a voice (Shippey). Born in 1892, two years after Angela Thirkell, Tolkien would surely admire Thirkell's Barsetshire, as English as The Hobbits' shire. Essentially, Thirkell wrote and lived in the same England where Tolkien wrote and lived. In *Love Among the Ruins,* Thirkell expresses her own "mythology for England" in the character of Lady Emily Leslie. As the academy finds a place for Tolkien's literary genius in its curriculum, it will be further rewarded by more scholarly attention to the world which Thirkell drew, out of her dedication to the cultural work of the English literary tradition.

Works Cited

Barry, Anita. *English Grammar: Language as Human Behavior*. 2nd ed. Upper Saddle River, NJ: Prentice Hall, 2002.

Barthes, Roland. *"To Write*: An Intransitive Verb?" *Structuralist Controversy*. Ed. Richard Macksey and Eugenio Donato. Baltimore: Johns Hopkins UP, 1972.

Benveniste, Emile. *Problems in General Linguistics*. Trans. Mary Elizabeth Meek. Coral Gables: U of Miami P, 1971.

Carpenter, Humphrey. *J.R.R. Tolkien: A Biography*. London: George Allen & Unwin Ltd, 1977.

Chance, Jane. *Tolkien's Art: 'A Mythology for England.'* Rev. ed. Lexington: UP of Kentucky, 2001.

Collins, Laura. *English Country Life in the Barsetshire Novels of Angela Thirkell*. Westport, CT: Greenwood, 1994.

Fritzer, Penelope. *Ethnicity and Gender in the Barsetshire Novels of Angela Thirkell*. Westport, CT: Greenwood, 1999.

Greenblatt, Stephen. "Racial Memory and Literary History." *PMLA* 116.1 (2001): 48-63.

Shippey, Thomas. *J.R.R. Tolkien: Author of the Century*. Boston: Houghton Mifflin, 2001.

Thirkell, Angela. *Love Among the Ruins*. Wakefield, RI: Moyer Bell, 1997 (originally published by Hamish Hamilton 1947).

Thirkell, Angela. *The Old Bank House*. Wakefield, RI: Moyer Bell, 1997 (originally published by Hamish Hamilton 1949).

Tompkins, Jane. *Sensational Designs: The Cultural Work of American Fiction 1790-1860*. New York: Oxford UP, 1985.

Williams, Raymond. *The Country and the City*. New York: Oxford UP, 1973.

Contributor

Mary Faraci earned her Ph. D. at the University of Florida and later studied modern criticism and theory with both Stanley Fish and Edward Said. She is the author of essays on the medieval style of criticism in the works of J. R. R. Tolkien, and on applying modern critical theory to medieval topics, including four articles accepted by the journal *Language and Style*. She has also published on Jane Austen and on Saul Bellow, and has presented a number of papers on linguistic approaches to literature. Her most recent publication is " 'I Wish to Speak': Tolkien's Voice in his Beowulf Essay" in the book *Tolkien the Medievalist*, edited by Jane Chance in 2003, and she will be presenting on "Tolkien and the Profession" at the 2005 Modern Language Association national conference. She is a Professor in the English Department at Florida Atlantic University, where she teaches British period courses, Linguistics and Literary Theory, Women in Literature, and Advanced Writing.

The Magpie Hoard
by
Cynthia Snowden

With her dark hair and intelligent bright eyes, Angela Thirkell might credibly be compared to a magpie—in the nicest possible way, of course. The magpie is reputed to find bright treasures and carry them to its nest for future reference. And this is exactly what Thirkell does in her writer's life: she uses a good education and years of voracious reading as a trove from which to withdraw treasures. She studs her fiction with those treasures—or in some cases bases it on them. Finding these treasures (or trying to find them) has been one delight for many readers of the Thirkell novels.

In reading and writing about the Barsetshire series, one can develop some idea of the contents of Angela Thirkell's figurative library, the cave or nest in which her treasures are stored. There is a growing sense of what she read, what books she loved, with what she was familiar. Yet, growing up a couple of generations later, on the other side of the Atlantic, many of today's readers naturally didn't read all the same things. If they had, they might know even more of what she borrowed. By accident in some cases and by following clues in other cases, it is possible to discover some of her magpie finds—surely not all. She was a devotee of Charles Dickens, William Shakespeare, Charlotte M. Yonge and Walter Scott, and equally well-read from a general assortment of contemporary literature—but her most obvious source of inspiration was Anthony Trollope.

Clearly the chief example of Thirkell's inspiration by Trollope is Barsetshire itself. Trollope created Barsetshire and its characters for his series of six Barsetshire novels: *The Warden, Barchester Towers, Doctor Thorne, Framley Parsonage, The Small House at Allington,* and *The Last Chronicle of Barset*, all of which appeared between 1855 and 1867. His Parliamentary, or Palliser, novels (*Can You Forgive Her?, Phineas Finn, The Eustace Diamonds, Phineas Redux, The Prime Minister,* and *The Duke's Children*), which appeared 1865-1880, are only partially set in Barsetshire, but some of the characters do have seats there. From this rich lode, Thirkell drew for almost thirty years, reviving the county of Barsetshire and peopling it with descendants of the characters created by Trollope.

Trollope laid the pattern of a pleasant, largely rural community of small villages surrounding the cathedral town of Barchester (presumably based on Salisbury), having as its focus the people of the church: bishop, deans, canons, precentors, vergers, and chaplains, as well as several of the Barsetshire landmarks with which readers are familiar: Framley Parsonage, Hogglestock, Boxall Hill, Greshamsbury, and the Cathedral Close, to name a few.

Any researcher must wonder how many of those reading the Thirkell books, or even this essay, have read all of Trollope, but following are some Trollope names in which some readers may recognize old friends: Bunce, Crawley, Crofts, Dale, de Courcey, Fothergill, Grantley, Gresham, Lufton, Omnium, Oriel, Palliser, Proudie, Scatcherd, Sowerby, Stringer, Thorne, and Umbleby.

Still, while Trollopian characters abound, they are not the principal ones. Mrs. Morland, of course, is not a character from Trollope, but is based on Thirkell herself. The Mertons, Keiths, Leslies, Warings, Birketts, Brandons, and Tebbens are examples of characters created by Thirkell, and as such owe no debt to Trollope.

The number of characters from Trollope picks up as the series progresses, possibly because referencing them was easier than making up new characters, or perhaps because it was an interesting challenge for Thirkell to revive them from those decades-old pages—after all, it seems logical to put the descendants of Trollope's characters into their home county. It is not easy to know just what sort of role Barsetshire played in Thirkell's life, but she must have found in it the same sort of welcoming respite from the real world that appeals to today's readers. And in that case, perhaps the Trollopian Barsetshire took on an aspect of reality that made it only reasonable to look in its villages and country houses for descendants from inhabitants of eighty years ago.

Reading through the list of characters, one may want to consider some of the names that are familiar from outside Barsetshire, as using them is so much a part of Thirkell's particular charm and humor. Lord Stoke's cook is named Mrs. Beeton, a wonderful name for a cook, since "Mrs. Beeton" has resonance in the culinary world, as well she might, having been the author of that widely-used nineteenth-century resource, *Household Management*. Sidney Carton, of course, is a character from Dickens' *Tale of Two Cities*. Feeder is from another Dickens novel, *Dombey and Son*. Lee Sumter, a gentleman from the American South, has a name redolent of the American Civil

War (Confederate General Robert E. Lee and Fort Sumter, the site of the beginning of the war). Donald Traill bears the same surname as another teacher, Archie Traill, from Hugh Walpole's grim novel *Mr. Perrin and Mr. Traill*. A comparison of the list of Thirkell characters to those of other writers shows several correspondences with Jane Austen, Charlotte M. Yonge, Walter Scott, and other mid-Victorian and Edwardian writers. Other treasures from the trove involve events, and the first example brings the reader back to Trollope.

In *August Folly,* a pivotal scene occurs involving Richard Tebben, the toddler Jessica Dean, and Rushwater Rubicon, the Leslies' bull (202-04). Richard, a rather gauche young man, is out for a walk with a few members of the Dean family. Jessica is sitting on Richard's donkey Modestine, which is led by her nanny. Rushwater Rubicon is on a professional visit to the Manor House, and has broken away from the cowmen who are chaperoning him; he trots "mildly bellowing" down the lane toward the approaching strollers. When Modestine stops suddenly, as donkeys are so apt to do, Jessica pitches forward and off. Richard, rolling her out of the way with his foot, puts himself and Modestine between the bull and the baby, and by this heroic deed earns the eternal gratitude of her father who expresses his thanks by providing, in years to come, a satisfying career opportunity for Richard.

This situation is a replaying of one in Trollope's *The Small House at Allington,* in which the gauche youth, Johnny Eames, saves Lord de Guest from his own bull (206-210). In gratitude, Lord de Guest becomes Johnny's mentor (people who are unimpressed by either of these scenes have obviously never seen a bull speeding toward them on their own side of the fence). Trollope's scene is long and earnest; Thirkell plays out her scene in a page and a half of clever writing.

In Trollope's Barsetshire series, Bishop Proudie of Barchester Cathedral is a weak man; Mrs. Proudie reigns in literary history as the villainess the reader loves to hate. It would defy common sense if Thirkell's bishop and his wife were anything other than direct descendants of this tradition. Throughout the series they are described in withering terms by all the Barcastrians, the bishop as weak and hen-pecked, his wife as disagreeable in every way, especially in her choice of hats. Not only is their church preference Low, their ways are mean, and an invitation to the Palace is dreaded before the fact, although discussed with some interest afterward, as people regale each other with accounts of the Palace's stinginess and cheese-paring ways.

A piece of large-scale borrowing from a different source has to do with the Harcourts and the Duke and Duchess of Towers, the names of characters from *Peter Ibbetson,* by George du Maurier. Without going into the plot of that rather peculiar novel—surely one of the more fantastic yet beguiling romances ever written—one can note that it features a lovely woman, the Duchess of Towers, whose husband's family name is Harcourt. It is as if Angela Thirkell, having read this novel, is unable to forget this captivating woman, and revives her in name if not in character. The names Harcourt and Towers are rather startling and jarring for being unlike any others in Barsetshire.

Another example from the hoard has to do with Wiple Terrace. *Invitation to the Waltz* by Rosamond Lehmann, contains the following description:

> Olivia . . . looked back at the slate roof, gable, tile and stucco façade, one of a row of three, the inscription CARRICKFERGUS in white glass lettering above the front door. The house on the right was called WINONA, the one on the left DUNDONALD. They were known in the family as Grandpapa's houses: for Grandpapa, that beneficent potentate, had built them, as well as the Parish Hall, in the same style. They stood aloof from the old, the picturesque, the in-Sanitary village proper— examples of modern improvement; and much local prestige attached to them.   (42)

Similarly, the earliest description of Wiple Terrace reads as follows:

> . . . a little terrace of four two-storied cottages in mellow red brick, with a wide strip of grass lying between them and the road. They were surmounted by a stucco pediment on which the words "Wiple Terrace" 1820 were visible. Mr. Wiple . . . was a small master builder of the village who had erected the terrace as a monument to his four daughters, Maria, Adelina, Louisa and Editha, calling each cottage after one of them.   (*Cheerfulness Breaks In* 80)

Perhaps such terraced properties abound in England, so this possible treasure from the trove will have to remain a speculation.

Not at all speculative is Thirkell's use of the phrase "a dainty rogue in porcelain," which she uses more than once to describe Clarissa Graham. The expression is from George Meredith's *The Egoist,* and is used by Mrs. Mountstuart Jenkinson to describe the young woman Clara Middleton to Clara's admirer, Sir Willoughby Patterne. Mrs. Mountstuart pronounces [Clara] to be "a dainty rogue in porcelain," and advises "I can imagine life-long amusement in her company. Attend to my advice: prize the porcelain and play with the rogue" (37-38).

A footnote in *The Egoist* advises that "rogue" has a second meaning in addition to its usual one of playful rascal: among ceramicists it indicates a crack or flaw (36). Applying the weight of both meanings, the reader can see that this description applies to Clarissa Graham. There probably remain many other examples of this sort of borrowed incident or concept to be discovered if researchers could read a complete list of the same books that Thirkell read. Another sort of literary borrowing that appears throughout the pages of the Barsetshire series, especially in the later books, is the use of direct quotation, indirect quotation, and allusion. Additionally, the use of foreign words and phrases could be considered a borrowing, although that claim might be a stretch.

In the case of direct quotations, such as bits of poetry or references to Shakespeare, sometimes the context reveals the source; often it does not. As a service to both the reader and the originator, many direct quotations are italicized or in quotation marks: in *Love at All Ages,* for example, Lord Pomfret quotes a passage from "Maud," by Alfred, Lord Tennyson (212). It is centered on the page, and there is no mystery as to its origin, who wrote it, or even that it is a quotation. In the case of other quotations, Thirkell doesn't make it so easy for the reader. In *Never Too Late,* the following passage appears:

The smiles, the tears of boyhood's years,
The words of love then spoken;
 The eyes that shone, now dimmed and gone,
 The cheerful hearts now broken.   (238)

These lines are an excerpt from "The Light of Other Days,"
a poem by Thomas Moore, set to music as "Oft in the Stilly
Night" and sung as some combination of lieder and folk
melody. One cannot know precisely how well known it was
during Angela Thirkell's formative or productive years, but
it was popular in certain circles—so popular that it took its
place in the web of culture with which "everyone" would
be familiar.

This reference brings up a critical point, necessary for
understanding any novel. There are songs and poems,
plays and novels, that are part of the culture prevailing in
any author's milieu, and few authors write with the idea in
mind that these songs, poems, plays, and novels will be so
unfamiliar to readers in the decades to come that references
to them will be baffling.

Even though Angela Thirkell did not go to university, she
was the daughter of a professor and had a very strong
education. In addition to governesses who taught her at
home, she attended both the Froebel Institute in Kensington
and St. Paul's School. Before she was finished, she had
studied Greek, Latin, French, German, Russian, history,
music, literature; she had written stories and poems, given
speeches, and acted in plays. She had spent some time in
Paris and in Gotha, Germany. By today's standards such an
education is rigorous, and would have left even a girl of
modest ability with a large stock of memorized poems,
favorite novels, lines from Shakespeare and foreign

expressions. This knowledge constituted the culture with which "everybody" (in Thirkell's particular circle) was acquainted. Angela Thirkell was so familiar with this body of cultural material that bits and pieces of it would naturally be present in her thinking much of the time—and she wove those bits and pieces into her work as naturally as she did her Trollope characters, apparently assuming that her readers would understand her references. Could a reader forget "Oft in the Stilly Night"? Impossible! Would Browning, Tennyson, Shakespeare, or Dickens ever cease to be known to "everyone"? Unthinkable! This assumption of knowledge is probably why so many of the quotations in Thirkell's work are not in quotation marks and are not attributed. She wasn't stealing work; rather, she was assuming the line was common knowledge.

In *Never Too Late,* there is a passage in French, quoted, not quite correctly, by George Knox :

> Je ne sais plus rien
> I see nothing more
> J'ai perds la mémoire
> I am losing my memory
> Du mal et du bien;
> Of the pain and of the good;
> O la triste histoire.
> O the sad story!   (*Never Too Late* 4)

This quote is from a poem known as "Une Grand Sommeil Noir" ("A Great Black Sleep") by Paul Verlaine, but there is absolutely nothing in the surrounding text to tip the reader off to that origin (*Selected Poems* 283*).* Does it matter if the reader misses this reference? Even if he or she can translate it pretty well— it's obviously about losing memory, even to those whose French is only first year—it adds depth, texture, and a bit of wry humor to know the deep coma-like despair that is the subject of the entire poem. Lack of context is one of the elements that is so annoying about missing things: one knows, on the basis of the things one does understand, how they enrich the experience of reading. Thirkell often slips in such subtle references, and readers are the losers if they don't recognize those references.

Indirect quotations are lines from another source, not attributed, nor in any way called attention to. So how does one know when they occur? The answer is, one doesn't, always. But one does develop a sense of when a line is just a bit unexpected, a tad different in tone, or when there is a mention of something extraneous, and one guesses that one is in the presence of an indirect quotation. Thirkell is by no means the only writer who does this—Dickens' work, for instance, is full of such lines—but it is a common practice of hers. One easy example appears on the first page of *Private Enterprise:*

> Since the glorious summer that marked the days of Dunkirk warmth and light had been withdrawn from England, and the peace, which had certainly passed everyone's understanding, had not the faintest influence on the weather, which had got the bit well between its teeth and was rapidly heading for the ice age.　　(1)

One can ignore the fact that the above paragraph is not a complete sentence, but has allowed its clauses to ravel out in some disarray. Also, one can ignore the well-known metaphor of the bit between the teeth that indicates something running away uncontrollably. What is left to examine is the "peace which had certainly passed everyone's understanding." To those familiar with church services, this is a line so well-known as to pass unnoticed, and it certainly will not be misunderstood. It is a Bible quotation, often used in benediction—Saint Paul addressing the Philippians: "The Peace of God, which passeth all understanding, shall keep your hearts and minds through Jesus Christ" (*Philippians* 4-7).

Later in the same novel is another indirect quotation:

> "Have you a little more of that delightful mixture? It is but rarely that I see the wine when it is red now," said Mr.Miller, eying the pale watery fluid that had to take the place of a proper cocktail.   (*Private Enterprise* 40)

Mr. Miller, as a man of the cloth, would of course be well acquainted with the relevant Biblical quotation:

> Look not thou upon the wine when it is red,
> When it giveth his colour in the cup,
> When it moveth itself aright
> And at the last it biteth like a serpent,
> And stingeth like an adder.   (*Proverbs* 23:29-32)

For the reader, knowing the source of these quotations increases the power and irony of their usage.

Allusion at its most simple is a reference to something outside the immediate context, as in this line found in *Never Too Late:*

> George, though at heart inclined to shout in his father's ear as Johnny Cake did to the Fox, came into the summer house and sat down on one of the rickety cane chairs.   (34)

The reader is presumed to know the story "Johnny Cake" from Joseph Jacobs' *English Fairy Tales*. Maybe English readers would, or those born in 1890. But neither of those conditions obtaining, the reader knows nothing, and has to guess. Such guessing is made no easier by the fact that in the U.S., johnnycake is a type of cornbread. Would the reader think of the Gingerbread Man? That is the closest he or she is likely to come in understanding this reference. Another example, from *Happy Return* is just as subtle:

'He made a translation of the first book of the Aeneid in rhyming couplets. Extremely bad they were,' after which array of facts almost worthy of Mr. F's aunt, the Dean said 'Ha,' and worked is mouth in a kind of grim smile, which softened as Simnet came in with Mr. Wickham's brandy. (70)

Mr. F's aunt? The reader may well be asking "Who is Mr. F?" Is he a character the reader somehow missed if he or she didn't read one of the earlier novels? No, no—but the reader is supposed to know that Mr. F is Mr. Finching, a (deceased) character from Dickens' *Little Dorritt*. His aunt, who is never known by her name, is a colorful character who makes her own cracked contribution to the novel, and to more than one of Thirkell's.

Thirkell also borrowed from her experiences, or from people she knew. Most writers deny that they do this, especially when it comes to characters, but literary biographies show that most authors borrow with wild abandon; indeed, such borrowing is a famous vehicle for an awful sort of revenge. And to the person who recognizes himself or a friend in a novel, the portrayal, however benign and well-meant, rarely seems felicitous. Thirkell ran into this problem when she used her family's friend, the Countess of Wemyss, as the model for Lady Emily. Later she created Miss Bunting, and based her very closely on the former governess Miss Bennet, who lived at Bere Court in Hampshire where Angela was the guest of Lady Helen Smith in 1941. In both these cases, the hostesses were outraged and the friendships ended (Strickland 87, 136).

It is very difficult for an author to write apart from his or her cultural context, and in most cases, it is the work of the reader to burrow into that rich soil to extract meaning. Thirkell is especially subversive in using references and pieces of quotations to carry messages that are somewhat saltier than they appear on the acceptable surface. Borrowing from previous authors is a literary tradition as old as literature itself. A form of it is experiencing a resurgence in recent years as contemporary authors take up where previous ones left off, or decide to re-tell a story in another way—rarely with the success of the original. But seldom has such literary intertwining been done with such thoroughness, or at such length, as Angela Thirkell has done it, building on the edifice created by Anthony Trollope and bringing it, in twenty-nine novels, into modern times. Thirkell lacks Trollope's interest in moral complexity, but she brings her bright treasure to his county and makes of it a place of peace and happiness, with residents whose lives unfold over the years in pleasant ways that continue to interest, charm, and amuse readers today.

Works Cited

Verlaine, Paul. "A Great Black Sleep" translated by Gertrude Hall in *Baudelaire, Rimbaud, Verlaine: Selected Verse and Prose Poems*. New York: Citadel Press, 1947.

Beeton, Isabella. *Beeton's Book of Household Management*. New York: Farrar, Straus and Giroux/The Noonday Press, 1977 (orig. 1861).

Dickens, Charles. *Dombey and Son*. New York: Oxford University Press, 1991 (orig.1847-48).

Dickens, Charles. *Little Dorritt*. New York: Oxford University Press, 1991 (orig. 1855-57).

Dickens, Charles. *A Tale of Two Cities*. New York: Oxford University Press, 1991(orig.1859).

Du Maurier, George. *Peter Ibbetson*. New York: Modern Library, 1932.

Jacobs, Joseph. *English Fairy Tales*. New York and London: G. P. Putnam's Sons, no date.

Lehmann, Rosamond. *Invitation to the Waltz*. New York, Harcourt, Brace & World, 1932.

Meredith, George, *The Egoist*. New York, The Modern Library, 1947.

Snowden, Cynthia. *Going to Barsetshire*. Kearney, Nebraska: Morris Publishing, 2000.

Strickland, Margo. *Angela Thirkell, Portrait of a Lady Novelist*. Kearney, Nebraska: Angela Thirkell Society of North America and Morris Publishing, 1996 (orig. 1977).

Thirkell, Angela. *August Folly*. New York, Carroll & Graf, 1988 (orig. 1936).

Thirkell, Angela. *Cheerfulness Breaks In*. New York, Alfred A. Knopf, 1941 (orig. 1940).

Thirkell, Angela. *Happy Return*. New York, Alfred A. Knopf, 1952.

Thirkell, Angela. *Love at All Ages*. New York, Alfred A. Knopf, 1959.

Thirkell, Angela. *Never Too Late*. New York, Alfred A. Knopf, 1956.

Thirkell, Angela. *Private Enterprise*. New York, Alfred A. Knopf, 1947.

Trollope, Anthony. *Barchester Towers*. London: The Folio Society, 1977 (orig. 1857).

Trollope, Anthony. *Can You Forgive Her?* London: Oxford University Press, 1973 [orig. 1864).

Trollope, Anthony. *Dr. Thorne*. Ware, England: Wordsworth Editions Ltd., 1994 (orig. 1861).

Trollope, Anthony. *The Duke's Children*. New York: Oxford University Press, 1973 (orig. 1880).

Trollope, Anthony. *The Eustace Diamonds*. New York: Oxford University Press, 1973 (orig. 1873).

Trollope, Anthony. *Framley Parsonage*. London: The Folio Society, 1978 (orig. 1861).

Trollope, Anthony. *The Last Chronicle of Barset*. London: The Folio Society, 1980 (orig. 1867).

Trollope, Anthony. *Phineas Finn*. New York: Oxford University Press, 1973 (orig.1869).

Trollope, Anthony. *Phineas Redux*. New York: Oxford University Press, 1973 (orig. 1874).

Trollope, Anthony. *The Prime Minister*. New York: Oxford University Press, 1973 (orig. 1876).

Trollope, Anthony. *The Small House at Allington*. London, The Folio Society, 1979 (orig. 1864).

Trollope, Anthony. *The Warden*. London: Oxford University Press, 1998 (orig. 1855).

Walpole, Hugh. *Mr. Perrin and Mr. Traill*. Harmondsworth, England: Penguin, 1938.

Contributor

Cynthia Snowden, of Sea Ranch, California, graduated with a B. A. in English and psychology from Southern Oregon College, and earned an M. S. in Rehabilitation Counseling from Indiana University. She is the author of *Going to Barsetshire*, a reference book on Thirkell's Barsetshire novels. She has been a member of the Angela Thirkell Society since 1994, and has several times addressed the membership at national conferences. She is widely read in authors contemporary to Thirkell, including E. M. Delafield, Rachel Ferguson, Elizabeth Jenkins, Joanna Cannan, and Mrs. Oliphant.

Morland and Barsetshire:
Thirkell's Metaliterary Worlds
by
Susan K. H. Kurjiaka

Angela Thirkell's early "Barsetshire" novels establish both young Tony Morland's status as an inventive, egotistical nuisance and Laura Morland's status as a writer of "second-rate" but marketable books. Thirkell's invention of her alter ego Mrs. Morland, widowed single mother to four boys, is a great addition to Anthony Trollope's world of Barsetshire, the imaginary literary locale about which that author wrote six novels in the nineteenth century, beginning with *The Warden* in 1855. The twenty-nine Thirkell "Barsetshire" works published from 1933-1961 bring the villages and descendants of Trollope's characters back to life, but also add other locations and people to the half-realistic, half-Romanticized English countryside.

However, the borrowing and remodeling take on a new literary life when Mrs. Morland's own works are described, read, or otherwise commented on in the course of the novels, becoming a rather wry commentary on authorship. Furthermore, there is another budding "litterateur"--the unflappable Tony, who not only manages a complete, ever-growing miniature railway land, but controls his very own imagined land, "Morland," taking over the idea from his young friend Dora, who thought of "Dorland" first, and accuses Tony (rightly) of copying her. The mixed roles of author, borrower, creator, and village controlling hand are also then being commented on in these Thirkell works. Both Laura and Tony Morland borrow and invent, paralleling Thirkell's purloining of Trollope's literary landscape. Furthermore, in addition to being commonly believed a re-creation of Thirkell's youngest son Lancelot (Lance), Tony Morland may represent Angela Thirkell's own literary imagination, as with a prolific outpouring of work she moved from single mothering and short literary pieces to establishing a strong reputation as a very popular novelist. She published at least one novel a year from 1931 to her death in 1961 (the day before her seventy-first birthday), when she left unfinished the last Barsetshire novel, *Three Score and Ten:*

> was completed from extensive notes by a friend and fellow writer, C[aroline]. A. Lejeune. Regardless of its provenance, it is a remarkable reprise of the whole series. Mrs. Morland (Thirkell's alter ego?), the protagonist of the first book . . . turns seventy affording the opportunity for a final gathering of our favorite people who continue to act as expected on all occasions. Young Robin Morland, son of the irrepressible Tony, helps or hinders or both at once.
>
> (Jacobucci 9)

About the penultimate Thirkell Barsetshire novel, *Love At All Ages* (1959), Amalia Jacobucci writes, "we are grateful, as always, that Thirkell, like Mrs. Morland, continues to write 'the same book' " (9). Thirkell's novels, set in a borrowed and expanded landscape, also include other levels of borrowing and commentary: her own alter ego Mrs. Laura Morland, creator of the (meta) literary world of Madame Koska, the fashion maven and sometime detective; and Tony Morland, the indefatigably verbose child who also invents an imaginary landscape and tells stories about it in his bossy way, riding roughshod over his friends until he gets his long trousers and enters the Upper

Form at school. He seems to leave his invented world behind when he (at age 13) says about Dora (age 12) and Rose (age 14) near the end of *The Demon in the House*, "'Those kids actually believe in Dorland and Morland, mother. But, of course, they're only kids'" (176). Here male privilege and the sheer egotistical force of Tony's personality and verbosity triumph over Rose's greater age. Thus the literary creative nature can comment on its own production, as Mrs. Morland does throughout Thirkell's series.

Since Mrs. Morland and Thirkell are both writers, the metaliterary aspects of the Barsetshire novels create another layer of meaning in the works. Metaliterary (or metafictional) is broadly defined by C. Hugh Holman and William Harmon as "beyond" fictional or literary; that is, fiction/literature that comments on itself or on the creative writing process by which it was formed. The autobiographical sources of both Tony and Laura Morland and the complex relationships to their respective imaginary worlds, as seen mainly in *High Rising* and *The Demon in the House* (which two early Barsetshire works establish Tony and especially Laura as central to the series), call for a metaliterary reading, as does *Growing Up*, in which Laura Morland lectures (however ironically) about her work and her way of creating it. These elements of Barsetshire and Morland and their metaliterary layers and characters are the subjects of this essay.

The first of Angela Thirkell's Barsetshire chronicles is *High Rising*, published in 1933, a year in which she also published two other works, *Ankle Deep* (not a Barsetshire book) and *Wild Strawberries*. Her well-received memoir, *Three Houses* (1931), had made a name for her two years earlier, as she had lovingly evoked her own idyllic childhood in art-filled studios and homes as a granddaughter of Sir Edward Burne-Jones, the Pre-Raphaelite artist, and as a cousin to Rudyard Kipling and his daughter Josephine, with whom Thirkell listened to Kipling's early versions of the *Just So Stories*. Here in Thirkell's first long work (although a relatively short memoir), she looked back nostalgically and rather romantically to her own innocent, privileged late-Victorian childhood (she was born in 1890 in London). Interestingly, she sometimes refers to herself as "the child" or "the girl," even though the work is told in the first-person narrative voice. These references to herself in the third-person narrative voice look forward to her use of "Laura Morland" as an autobiographically derived alter ego.

This privileged high-society, artist- and intellectual-filled late-nineteenth-century "Gilded Age" period gave way, however, to a very twentieth-century adulthood, with two unsuccessful marriages, the loss of an infant daughter (three sons survived), two World Wars, experience as a single mother to at least one difficult young son, and household moves from England to Australia and back. The changes in Thirkell's own life led to the contemporaneous themes, plots, and genteel characters with which she fills the Barsetshire novels, and which were already disappearing by the time of her death.

Already a mother of two sons (Graham, born 1912; Colin, born 1914) and a daughter (Mary, born 1917) by her first husband James McInnes, whom she divorced in 1917, Angela Margaret Mackail McInnes ("Life" 1) met and married George Lancelot Thirkell in 1918, the same year her daughter Mary died. The Thirkells traveled on a troopship in 1920 to his hometown in Australia. Later, "their adventures on the 'Friedricksruh' are recounted in

her *Trooper to the Southern Cross* published in 1934"
("Life" 1), under the pseudonym Leslie Parker. "Partly
because of a desire to write and partly because of a need to
earn money, Thirkell began writing short stories while
living in Melbourne" (Commire 384), and had some
success publishing for periodicals in both Australia and
England.

However, after her husband's business failed at the
beginning of the Great Depression in 1929, she left
Australia, taking young Lance Thirkell (age eight) back to
her parents' home in London. After the success of her
memoirs in 1931, she came upon her niche: borrowing,
reinventing and re-peopling Trollope's Barsetshire, and
chronicling the lives, manners, and marriages of her
middle-and upper-class country contemporaries, somewhat
like a twentieth-century Jane Austen. "In 1933, readers
saw a virtual explosion of novels from Thirkell" (Commire
384).

The novels' connections with country life and manners, the
art and literary scene, are all autobiographical--but so was
the need to make money and support her sons (Thirkell and
Mrs. Morland share the same necessity). Her choice to be a
professional writer was made at least partly because
Thirkell "badly needed to earn a living" ("Life" 1). As
stated about Mrs. Morland in *High Rising*, Thirkell's work
also "suited the public taste, and . . . Laura had educated
Gerald and John, and got Dick into the navy, and now there
was really no anxiety and only the inscrutable Tony to be
dealt with. She . . . never took herself seriously, though she
took a lot of trouble over her books" (*High Rising* 14).

Another reason for writing was clearly talent. Immediately
after the above quotation, Thirkell has Laura modestly

think about her successes: "If she had been more introspective, she might have wondered at herself for doing so much in ten years, and being able to afford a small flat in London, and a reasonable little house in the country, and a middle-class car" (*High Rising* 14)--plus household help in the form of Stoker, and even a secretary, which Laura believes is a true mark of success.

The interconnectedness and continuity (however imperfect) of the Barsetshire novels compel readers to look overall at this period of 1933-1960 during which Thirkell imagines modern British life in her own gently ironic quiet way. This intertextuality points to the many metaliterary aspects of the texts, as Thirkell translates life in a world-wide depression and in a world war (and its aftermath) into a world of genteel manners, where although she "uses a great deal of autobiographical material . . . she always stopped short of the truly unpleasant" (Collins 88). Indeed, Laura Morland and Angela Thirkell both are quintessential "ladies," which idea Margot Strickland references for the title of her biography, *Angela Thirkell, Portrait of a Lady Novelist* (1977), where "Lady Novelist" hints at the nature of both the author and her main character, and to the other characters, ladies and gentlemen mostly, the "upstairs" gentry with a few "downstairs" folk thrown in for good measure.

In another parallel between Thirkell and Mrs. Morland, the early "Barsetshire" novels establish Tony Morland's status as not only a nuisance but also a recreation of Thirkell's youngest son Lance Thirkell. *High Rising* introduces the reader not only to Mrs. Morland, but also to the youngest of her four boys, Tony (who is about twelve--the same age as Lance in 1933), their friends, neighbors, household help, villagers, and his school and her publisher.

In Angela Thirkell's first Barsetshire novel, she sets the plot pattern that will be played out in most of her later books. She also introduces us to specific characters as well as "types" who will appear and reappear in changing relationships as the years go by. There is the middle-aged woman centrally involved in the events and activities around her; here, Laura Morland, a happily widowed author of very successful "good bad books" (Thirkell herself?). . . . Especially delightful are the children, servants, and other retainers; well defined characters in their own right; from motor-mouthed young Tony Morland and his model railways to the housekeeper, Stoker, and her grapevine among the servants of the neighborhood.   (Jacobucci 1)

The Demon in the House, the third Barsetshire novel, is sometimes referred to as a collection of short stories, composed as it is around the calendar of Tony Morland's school holidays. The chapters (or story titles?) are numbered and titled "1. The Easter Holiday," "2. The Half-term Holiday," "3.The Summer Holidays," and "4. The Christmas Holidays." Although the Morlands have a small flat in London, Mrs. Morland prefers to be in the country and close to Tony's school during the vacations.

During the series, Thirkell takes the original nineteenth-century Barsetshire setting into the post-Edwardian, post-"Great War" times. Writing throughout the 1930s, 1940s and 1950s, she chronicles the realistic nature of contemporaneous British country life and the incredible changes the people must go through. However, emotionally realistic hardships are downplayed in favor of engagements and marriages and gentle humor while people mostly uncomplainingly "carry on." Thirkell matures these domestic chronicles through the Depression, World War II (as wars began to be numbered), and its aftermath among the gentry of Trollope's imaginary shire, now peopled with both descendants of his characters and her own interlopers.

It is no wonder that along with her reimagining and expansion of Trollope's world, Thirkell adds a wry commentary on her own literary borrowing by having young Tony purloin, use, and later discard, an imaginary land of which he is very jealous and possessive. Stolen from his friend Dora's idea of "Dorland," the world of "Morland" resounds with metafictional commentary on Thirkell's own invented and reinvented worlds. In *The Demon in the House*, twelve-year-old Dora Gould is the vicar's child, who--with a mind of her own--is an "unhappy exception" to the now thirteen-year-old Tony's need for friends with "an infinite capacity to listen to what he said," although her sister Rose, a year older than Tony, is content with a small section of Tony's world called "Rosebud" (4). Dora "talked a great deal about an imaginary country called Dorland, after herself...In self-defense Tony had been obliged to create a country of his own, which he called Morland" (5):

> He broke the news of this country to Rose and Dora when they were all upstairs in Tony's playroom one day.
>
> "You're copying me," said Dora indignantly, on hearing of Morland.
>
> "I'm not. Morland is a real name; and as a matter of fact it was called after us hundreds of years ago. Dorland is just a silly make-up name."
>
> (*The Demon in the House* 5)

The children compete over who has the highest mountain, but Tony talks circles around Dora and then changes the subject. Later, he tells her that all the new inventions come first to Morland, because it is not only older but more advanced than the paltry Dorland. Thirkell seems to be using Tony to say that if one is able to, and talks (writes?) fast enough, one is allowed to purloin an imaginary world and to expand it--and to even make it one's own creation, even if the idea was not original to the current imaginer. Certainly this is what Thirkell did with Trollope's Barsetshire, writing twenty-nine novels in her series over twenty-eight years, compared to Trollope's original six novels over twelve years. Trollope's series began in 1855 and continued through *The Last Chronicle of Barset*, published in 1867. Although he, too, was a prolific and well-respected novelist, "In his later novels Trollope shifted his interest from the rural scene to urban society and politics" ("Trollope" 1).

In another metaliterary parallel, Thirkell's series centers around the supposedly "second-rank" novelist Laura Morland. In turn, Mrs. Morland inhabits Barsetshire while herself writing about yet another invented world of mystery, melodrama, and seduction, the atelier and work of *her* heroine, Madame Koska, the high-fashion maven and mystery-solver. Thirkell's narrator explains this choice of subject:

> Laura had written for magazines for some years past, in a desultory way, but now the problem of earning money was serious. She had considered the question carefully, and decided that next to racing, murder and sport, the great reading public of England (female section) liked to read about clothes. With real industry she [. . .

studied the subject] and settled down to write best-sellers. Her prevision was justified, and she now had a large, steady reading public, who apparently could not hear too much about the mysteries of the . . . clothes business.   (*High Rising* 13)

Thirkell continues to explain Mrs. Morland's invented world of the fashion thriller with a description of one of her "potboiler" fictions, "which had even been dramatized with considerable success, its central scene being the workroom of the famous Madame Koska," where the handsome French traveler was recognized as a former lover that a rival's young infiltrator had robbed and left years ago: Thirkell describes the melodramatic story as "all too long and improbable to relate. But, most luckily, it suited the public taste" (13-14). Of course, Thirkell is mocking the sensationalism of thrillers while also establishing that she has a right--like Laura Morland--to do whatever she wants with the literary world she has created (even if at first borrowed). She has certainly made it her own. As Laura Collins writes,

Mrs. Thirkell's yearly novels are mild chronicles of rural English life, dealing with the varied population of the whole county and spiced with the author's sharp and sometimes slightly malicious wit, while Mrs. Morland's Madame Koska series provides variations on the highly improbable goings-on in that lady's business establishment, where international espionage and smuggling vie with unscrupulous efforts of Madame Koska's rivals to pirate her *haute couture* collections.
                                                                              (90)

Thus to Trollope's Barsetshire Thirkell adds the Morlands, who both invent their own imaginative worlds, one of literature and one of play--or it is both of play? Within one of the Morlands' worlds, the world of Madame Koska appears, like another "play within a play." Is it an accident that Thirkell uses Trollope's own given name--Anthony--for Laura's mischievous fourth son? And how handy for a youngster to have a name ending in -*land*, especially when he must quickly create a country in order to stay on top of his game! Of course, "Morland" is both Tony's imaginative world within his supposed world of Barsetshire, and his and his mother's surname. Thus even the name has immediate metafictional qualities.

Because Angela Thirkell filled her novels with writers, publishers, readers, talkers, intellectuals, schoolmasters and schoolboys, and comments on other works and writers such as Shakespeare, Dickens, Browning, Tennyson, and Thirkell's contemporary and friend John Buchan (Macdonald 2-3), the characters may be envisioned as commenting both within the text on Mrs. Morland and her writing, and pointing outside the text to comment on Thirkell herself and her work, in a kind of metaliterary world-in-world. The comments about Mrs. Morland's writing, which she often makes herself, are also often about both her son and her books--how (well) did she raise one (or four?) and write the other(s)? In addition to the metaliterary aspects involved, all these layers and parallels point up the autobiographical aspects of Thirkell's work.

Lance Thirkell himself resisted the implication that because of his mother's description of Mrs. Morland's distracted "dislike" (*Growing Up* 244) of and impatience with Tony, her own "mothering" was in any way faulty. He edited "a collection of excerpts from her letters" titled *Baby, Mother, and Grandmother* (Collins 67). Angela Thirkell had written letters from Australia to her own mother in England

(Lance's "grandmother" of the above title--he is the baby) in the 1920s, describing her life with her infant third son far from the "three houses" and family in and around London. Later, supposedly upset with criticism of his mother or of the faulty parenting attributed to Laura Morland and thus to her creator, Angela Thirkell, he privately published these letters in 1982 to show her kindnesses in her mothering of him ("Books" 4). The volume is evidence that she was a devoted, loving mother to Lance, and as Laura Collins says, "the author had had the wonderful and satisfactory experience of being a loving mother to the child of a loved husband" (115). However, the changes Thirkell underwent, with her husband losing his business and her removing to England without him, experiencing "single motherhood" at her parents' home in London with her eight-year-old, would surely have put stresses on even the best of mother-son relationships. Indeed,

> Tony and the many babies and children of various ages depicted in her novels reveal her understanding of and affection for the young, but in the books she never left alone the interrelationships of children of whatever age, and their parents. This life-long examination reveals that whatever mistakes she made as a parent she brooded over, seriously, for a long period, and eventually saw with much clarity the offspring's view, as well as that of the parent; and although she had sometimes found it impossible to be the loving or the wise parent, she recognized such parents, and the reader meets them in her novels. (Collins 115)

Much has been made of Tony Morland's character as an endearing but obnoxious, self-aggrandizing child, especially in these early two Barsetshire novels, *High Rising* and *The Demon in the House,* where Tony and his mother are the central characters. He is a lower-form "public school" (Americans' "private school") student at Southbridge school, on the southwest side of Barsetshire, thirty or forty miles from the eastern village of High Rising, where Laura has a country cottage. In *The Demon in the House*, the living and financial arrangements and the mother-son relationship are the first things narrated, and closely tied with the mother's writing of books: "When Tony Morland wasn't at school he lived with his mother in the country" (1). "As his three elder brothers were usually abroad or at sea, he missed the fraternal snubbing which is supposed to improve the character. His mother sometimes tried to be a little unkind to him, because she felt the responsibility of being a father and mother rolled into one, but she wasn't very successful" (1). Thirkell continues:

> His mother wrote books to earn enough money to have a house in the country and send Tony to school. Tony had read some of her books, but did not think very highly of them. . . . But luckily Laura Morland didn't in the least mind what Tony thought of her books, nor what any one else thought, so long as she could please the people who get books from the libraries. And luckily for Tony, the library people liked his mother's books much better than he did.
>
> (*The Demon in the House* 1-2)

Thus in the first few pages Laura Morland is shown as perhaps more comfortable and successful with her writing than with her parenting. Of course, one element is necessary for making a living, and the other for loving, and she is clearly able to do both, as was Thirkell. Laura Morland is widowed, while Angela Thirkell had had three children with one marriage lasting seven years, and one child in a stronger happier relationship, which, however, also ended in the couple splitting, when she left him in Australia in 1929 and never returned.

One critic has said that "the attractively harassed Mrs. Morland sees right through her exasperating son Tony, but really enjoys indulging his boyish obsessions" (Collins 65). But in Mrs. Morland's exasperation one sees a deprecation of Thirkell's own mothering, about which she clearly (if one reads autobiographically) has mixed feelings and anxieties. If one reads with a metaliterary focus, looking for clues to attitudes about writing and writers, Mrs. Morland's confusion as a mother seems to be mirrored in a similar confusion about her writing. In the novels, her work is put down, joked about, called "second rate," and just generally not taken seriously--especially by Laura herself. For example, in the later novel *Growing Up* (1943), Mrs. Morland goes to give a lecture to "some forty or fifty convalescent soldiers" (239). The third-person omniscient narrator, looking over Laura Morland's shoulder, tells us Laura's thoughts, beginning with the wish that she had never been born:

She hated any kind of public appearance and had only twice spoken to an audience, in both cases at the request of her publisher with whom she had almost quarreled afterwards owing to general nervous misery . . . . If her own sons were anything to judge by, the very last thing they would want was to have a middle-aged woman with no allure coming and talking to them about how she wrote books. . . . Mrs. Morland had accepted [the subject because] she could be just as stupid about that as about anything else. . . . How on earth could one expect . . . soldiers, to read what were really only potboilers? Thrillers about Madame Koska, in whose dress-making establishment her readers demanded to meet a new hero, heroine, female spy and foreign secret agent every year, sandwiched with descriptions of clothes and the difficulties of a fashionable dressmaker, seemed to her the last thing in the world for military circles. (239)

One cannot write all that Thirkell had written by 1943 and not have some tongue-in-cheek words kept to herself. Indeed, although Mrs. Morland hates lecturing, even close to home, Thirkell herself "did take some time off from her busy writing schedule in 1949, however, to travel to the United States and give lectures at Yale and Columbia universities" (Commire 384). After almost two decades of dealing with Barsetshire and the last four years with England at war, Thirkell has Mrs. Morland later in the soldiers' lecture state, "'You see, my publisher *will* make me write books . . . so then I get so furious . . . . And then I sit down, very angrily, and write a book'" (*Growing Up* 241). This is as much of an analysis of writing as Mrs. Morland wants to do, and she spends the rest of the dreaded lecture time talking about her three eldest boys.

Thirkell's sharp pen, however, is looking for a more pointed commentary about writing, and soon has one. In *Growing Up*, Laura's host Sir Harry suggests that she'll have them all in a book soon enough, and Thirkell's description of Laura's spinning authorial mind is hilarious: "Mrs. Morland was trying to forget the remark about putting people in books, a suggestion which always drove her to frenzy and to a strong wish to tell the speaker that no one present was either interesting or funny enough to find their way into a book of hers" (245), showing the healthy respect of Thirkell (and Mrs. Morland!) for the author/character/self. Since this conversation takes place in a book set in 1943, perhaps her respect for her own work has grown in the past decade, in this twelfth Barsetshire book.

By the time *Growing Up* is published, the character of Tony has matured into a charming--very charming and manipulative--young army officer. His mother explains to the men that she didn't purposefully attempt to be an author. She says, "You see, when my husband died I wasn't very well off and I had four boys, so I simply had to do something. I didn't ever *mean* to write books" (*Growing Up* 242). She also talks about her three eldest, but is interrupted before she can discuss Tony. In any case, Tony himself is there (or expected in one minute to pick up his Mother), as is the Dr. Ford from the first two novels (in which he only said "Shut up" to Tony). Thirkell hints at these complicated relationships: "Dr. Ford had always been one of Tony's sharpest critics, and Tony's mother, who adored and disliked her youngest son to distraction, did not wish her old friend to have a righteous cause of displeasure against him" (*Growing Up* 244). Once again, all the interrelationships are juxtaposed and become complex metaliterary commentaries not only on personalities but also on the process of writing and creating new worlds within old.

The worlds-within-world that Angela Thirkell is able to create thus are satisfying and entertaining for a number of reasons. She is witty and wise, and creates an autobiographical central character who is sharp, funny, very human, and even self-deprecating, although with a limit to what she will accept and a deep sense of what is upright and well-mannered behavior. Thirkell's chronicles give an extraordinary picture of a now-vanished era in British history as the countryside moved (rather painfully even if humorously) up through the era of Queen Elizabeth II. While remaining popular and even gaining in popularity, especially in the United States with the reprinting of many of her works, Thirkell was also a well-respected novelist whose works have excellent literary techniques, fine characterization, gentle humor, an observant eye, and layers of meaning including autobiographical and metafictional concerns. The Barsetshire novels merit, and undoubtedly will continue to collect, a growing body of criticism.

Works Cited

Angela Thirkell Society. "Angela Thirkell's Books" ("Books"). 1-5. http://www.ngelathirkell.org/atbooks.htm. 12/20/2004.

Angela Thirkell Society. "Angela Thirkell's Life" ("Life"). 1-2. http://www.angelathirkell.org/ atbio.htm. 12/20/04.

Collins, Laura Roberts. *English Country Life in the Barsetshire Novels of Angela Thirkell.* Westport, CT: Greenwood Press, 1994.

Commire, Anne. Ed. "Thirkell, Angela (1890-1961)." *Women in World History: A Biographical Encyclopedia.* Vol. 15. Waterford CT: Yorkin Publications, 2002. 383-384.

Holman, C. Hugh, and William Harmon. *A Handbook to Literature.* Sixth Edition. New York: MacMillan Publishing Company, 1992.

Jacobucci, Amalia Angeloni. "Angela Thirkell Book Summaries." http://www.angelathirkell.org/atbrief.htm. 11/12/2004.

Macdonald, Kate. "Angela Thirkell and John Buchan." Webpage copyright @ The John Buchan Society 2004. http://www.johnbuchansociety.co.uk/thirkell.htm. 12/23/04.

Strickland, Margot. *Angela Thirkell, Portrait of a Lady Novelist.* n.p.: Duckworth, 1977.

Thirkell, Angela Mackail. *The Demon in the House.* Wakefield RI: Moyer Bell, 1996 [orig.1934].

Thirkell, Angela. *Growing Up.* Wakefield RI: Moyer Bell, 1996, [orig. 1943].

Thirkell, Angela. *High Rising.* New York: Carroll & Graf Publishers, Inc., 1989 [orig. 1933].

Thirkell, Angela. *Three Houses.* Oxford & London: Oxford UP, 1931.

Thirkell, Lance. *Baby, Mother, and Grandmother.* Privately published, 1982. Listed at http://www.angelathirkell.org/atbooks.htm. 12/20/ 2004.

"Trollope, Anthony." *The Columbia Encyclopedia, Sixth Edition.* New York: Columbia UP, 2004.
http://www.bartleby.com/65/tr/Trollope.html.

Contributor

Susan Kurjiaka earned her B. A. and M. A. in English from the University of Massachusetts at Amherst and her Ph. D. in English from the University of North Carolina at Chapel Hill. In 1994 she won her first teaching award and also was a National Endowment for the Humanities Summer Scholar at Yale University. She taught for a year at the University of Warsaw in Poland as a Fulbright fellow. She has published and presented on Emily Dickinson, Nathaniel Hawthorne, Walt Whitman, Thomas Hardy, slave narratives, F. Scott Fitzgerald, and other writers. She is a tenured Associate Professor in the English Department at Florida Atlantic University, where she teaches courses in American Literature, late Nineteenth and early Twentieth-century British Literature, and Women's and Ethnic Literature. Currently she is researching the connections between Harriet Beecher Stowe, Harriet Jacobs, and Harriet Wilson.

Northbridge Rectory in Wartime
by
A. J. Minogue

In *Northbridge Rectory*, Angela Thirkell paints a charming picture of life on the home front during World War II. There are many interesting elements in Thirkell's portrayal, and one of the most striking and amusing attributes of the novel is that the characters have little or no actual interest in the war itself, although it is a constant part of their daily lives. They rarely discuss politics, their country's enemies, any specific casualties, or the war's potential outcomes. Instead, they discuss matters of daily life, mentioning the war only as it applies to them on a personal level. Mrs. Villars, the novel's protagonist, explains how the demands of daily life take precedence over the details of the war, because the characters' attention is diverted by having to constantly hunt for food in the shops and to collect money for the National Saving, among a myriad of other activities, activities that take up a lot of time and concentration (185).

At a dinner party at the Villars' home, the Northbridge residents in attendance discuss the contents of their emergency kits. The neighborhood intellectuals, Miss Pemberton and Mr. Downing, keep copies of their unfinished manuscripts and their sweaters. Mrs. Villars gathers together her silk stockings and her passport each evening. Mr. Villars, Northbridge's somewhat secular rector, tells his guests that his emergency kit holds a spare set of false teeth and a Bible, and then regrets mentioning the Bible after the false teeth (93-94). Certainly, these characters would not have emergency kits if there were not a war on, but the items they choose reflect their priorities (comfort and a little luxury) and their personal identities (the writers' manuscripts and the vicar's Bible). The war kits do not suggest that the characters are very afraid. If anything, they are just nervous enough to make emergency kits, but not nervous enough to actually prepare for an emergency.

These makeshift emergency kits certainly are not designed nor assembled in accordance with any official government ordinance or suggestions. England at the time advised her citizens to store buckets of water and sand, and the government distributed assemble-yourself bomb shelters at the time the novel takes place. A few younger characters store water and sand, but fail to gather any sentimental items together. While they are more interested in stocking actual emergency supplies, the fact that they don't gather any personal items again indicates that they don't believe there is a real threat that they might need to evacuate their homes. In all cases, the guests at Mrs. Villars' home that evening, like all their neighbors, do not indicate that they are truly afraid through their behaviors. Similarly, after the 9-11-01 attacks, when President Bush's staff advised New Yorkers to stock up on duct tape, many filled their emergency kits, if they had them at all, with sentimental items and/or bottles of fine wine.

The British countryside during World War II and post 9-11-01 New York City are worlds apart in many regards, but once the specific politics, enemies, casualties and outcomes are put aside (as they are in Thirkell's novel), the experiences of the people of Northbridge and those of countless New Yorkers are quite similar. People in harm's way are frightened to varying degrees, but they tend to treasure their memories, their comforts, and their senses of humor. Most of all, maintaining a way of life - manners, routines, social obligations - is essential to surviving the stresses of the home front.

However, real-life English people's behaviors did not always align with the behaviors of the countryside characters of *Northbridge Rectory*. The oral history of Jean Wood, a woman who evacuated from London to the English countryside during World War II is an example. As recorded in *The Good War: An Oral History of World War II* by Studs Terkel, Mrs. Wood recalls the difficulty she had trying to maintain life as usual. She notes, "You'd hear the bomb drop so many hundreds yards away. And you'd think, Oh, that missed us. You'd think, My God, the next one's going to be a direct hit. But you'd continue to read ["Cinderella" to her children]: 'And the ugly sister said' - and you'd say, 'Don't fidget, dear.' And you'd think, My God, I can't stand it" (Terkel 216). As in *Northbridge Rectory*, maintaining the routines of daily life is essential; however, in Mrs. Wood's account, the threat was perceived to be real, and maintaining daily life routines required a great deal more effort.

Mrs. Villars is comparatively unafraid, and for her, daily life is fairly easily maintained, aside from the intrusion of having people quartered in the house. One possible reason the experiences and attitudes of Mrs. Villars and Mrs. Wood are so different may be that they had very different husbands. The fictional Mrs. Villars' husband served in World War I and is now a level-headed vicar. Mr. Villars, who has no particular role on the home front in World War II, consistently "saves" Mrs. Villars. For reasons not explained in *Northbridge Rectory*, Mr. Villars demands that his wife rest every afternoon. These seemingly frivolous naps may very well be the key to her sanity. She maintains a comforting routine and as a result is capable of serving as the reader's semi-objective ambassador into the lives of her neighbors. Mrs. Villars shares with the reader her private resentments of overachieving wartime volunteers and the imposition of house guests (the British officers assigned to her home), and rationing, with a bit more joy and wise distance than her non-napping neighbors. The reader learns that her older son is a Professor of Engineering "required to stick to his job," and her second son in the Air Force is "entirely engaged on instruction," so she never displays any anxiety about their safety (29). She is, like her husband, calm and content in her role.

In contrast, the real-life Mrs. Wood's husband was younger, and he voluntarily enlisted in the army shortly after the couple evacuated from London. During the war, Mrs. Wood takes care of their small children and fears for the safety of her husband, children, and herself, sometimes in the unwelcoming homes of others. Consequently, when comparing and contrasting the experiences of the two women, it is important to note their very different emotional lives. That being said, both women describe starkly different wartime volunteering stories.

Although she considers the social benefits of volunteering, Mrs. Villars cannot become an active wartime volunteer because she respects her husband's instructions to rest every afternoon (*Northbridge Rectory* 45). However, neither Mr. nor Mrs. Villars is able to escape participating in the "women's spotters" project assigned by Northbridge's

Air Warden (41). The participants (the town's women, Mr. Villars, and Mr. Downing) break up into pairs to observe the town from the church's tower and report anything suspicious. Mrs. Villars wryly recounts, towards the middle of the novel, the uselessness of this exercise: "No one denied that excellent work had been done by the roof-spotters, from Betty, who distinctly saw... a pied gobble-belly trying to nest out of season .... [to] Miss Dunsford ...[who] was able to give valuable evidence in the matter of a mild collision between Captain Topham's little car and an army lorry which was pulling at a highly illegal speed and on the wrong side of the road" (*Northbridge Rectory* 165).

Mrs. Villars summation of the volunteering effort is clearly not universal. While many volunteers never saw any danger, many did, including Mrs. Wood, who volunteered for a similar volunteer post. "I did fire-watch. And that's frightening. You got up on the roof with a steel helmet on. You're supposed to have a protective jacket. The fire bombs are round balls. They'd come onto roofs and start fires. So the government gave you a bucket of sand and a shovel. Charming. (Laughs.) You stood there till the bomb fell. And you'd shovel it up quick and throw it into the bucket of sand" (Terkel 216).

The personalities of volunteers, as well as their experiences, shape their wartime roles. While Mrs. Villars does little volunteering and doesn't particularly value the experience, and Mrs. Wood's fire-watching experience was more dangerous, but not necessarily very time-demanding, Mrs. Paxon of *Northbridge Rectory* does more than any other woman in the novel, and perhaps more then any real woman in World War II England. The town's busybody, Mrs. Paxon is capable, conscientious, and exhausting to be around. While Mrs. Villars admires her, it is also clear that amongst the praise there is a tinge of resentment. Maybe Mrs. Paxon is resented for her energy, or maybe for obviously taking the war seriously. She has so many volunteer duties, including dealing with "evacuees, refugees, air-raid precautions, auxiliary fire service, personal service... the Red Cross; housed by a miracle of congestion her husband's two aunts and an evacuated mother with twins; collected National Savings; was billeting officer for the Plashington Road, and went to early [church] service three days in the week," that she is often seen wearing different pieces of several different uniforms (*Northbridge Rectory* 27). When Mrs. Paxon comes to call on Mrs. Villars, Mrs. Paxon is wearing an odd assortment of garments by which Mrs. Villars tries to guess to which war activity Mrs. Paxon has either been or is going (38).

When visiting, Mrs. Paxon is courteous, but always has the war on her mind. While Mrs. Paxon's behaviors are exhausting, giving Mrs. Villars cause to roll her eyes, she never actually does. Rather, Mrs. Villars refrains from such behavior because she truly admires Mrs. Paxon's ability to keep up with her domestic obligations. Despite her countless volunteering activities, Mrs. Paxon always has a clean home and a well-fed husband. Mrs. Villars fears that if she herself volunteered more, she would neither be a good volunteer nor maintain her comfortable home life (which includes those guests foisted upon her, whom she nevertheless treats graciously, even inviting Major Spender's wife, when she wants to visit her husband but has no place to stay) (58). Instead of doing both badly, Mrs. Villars naps and stays close to home.

The tension between domestic responsibilities and wartime responsibilities combined with the absence of husbands serving in the military in many homes changed the roles of women in England. Women were gaining an identity outside of the home and in some cases earning money for the first time in new wartime women's services positions. Through Mrs. Paxon's character, Thirkell conservatively resists this change by praising her character most for never sacrificing her husband's domestic comforts. Only once does Mrs. Villars hint that Mrs. Paxon's behavior may contribute to her "collapse" (Mrs. Paxon finally gets influenza and has to rest at The Aloes), and that her household may have been overly dependent on her energy, because Miss Dolly Talbot agrees to volunteer to be the woman of the Paxon household and do the shopping and cooking (265). While Thirkell admits here that Mrs. Paxon took on too much, Thirkell treats Mrs. Paxon's domestic responsibilities as a full time role worthy of Miss Talbot's serious attention, suggesting that it is Thirkell's opinion that English women not belittle the position of lady-of-the-house as any less valuable or demanding than the new wartime roles.

Thirkell may be suggesting that most wartime volunteering is for younger women. Mrs. Turner's nieces are involved in a number of wartime activities, and show their enthusiasm and the frivolity of the activities by rushing off to ARP posts to get the better camp-bed (100) and heartily resenting missing a V. A. D. post in Tube Shelters because of influenza (267). This youthful enthusiasm is meant to be endearing when it comes from young women, but it would be unbecoming to the rector's wife or even to Mrs. Paxon. Throughout all the Barsetshire novels, too much enthusiasm is always presented as vulgar. The above-referenced nieces, who are presented as perfect for wartime volunteering assignments, also are consistently portrayed as lower middle class. Unlike the other characters of Northbridge, the nieces consistently say words like "ackcherly," in Thirkell's purposeful attempt to make them appear less polished by emphasizing their accents. The reader is left to conclude that if one is not young, lower middle class, or a superwoman like Mrs. Paxon, it is best to go about one's business with as few wartime involvements as possible.

However, one cannot avoid the effects of war altogether. While one can minimize the amount of volunteering she does, no one can completely ignore the impact of war on daily life. For instance, the air-raid sirens are a consistent reminder. They worry the most steadfast, including Mr. and Mrs. Villars, whose sleep is somewhat affected by the sirens. Even the ordinarily unemotional Miss Pemberton rushes home while the sirens blast because she doesn't like the idea of her "house being alone in a raid" (*Northbridge Rectory* 113). However, the sirens, much like the current U. S. color-coded "Homeland Security Advisory System," hardly seem very relevant in day-to-day life. While the citizens of Northbridge respond dutifully to their volunteer posts when they hear an air-raid siren, they doubt the sirens' reliability, as shown by Father Fewling's remark, "Well, you know our siren. Never yet has she let loose with any relation to anything that is happening" (260).

The bomb shelters themselves are invariably homey, not only in Northbridge, but also in real life. Mrs. Wood reports that "They had public underground shelters... We also had our own air-raid shelter that the government issued... Such was the fortitude of the ordinary working class that they made little cozy living rooms in it. (Laughs)" (Terkel 214). Likewise, the Northbridge Warden's Shelter seems more like a cozy secret children's fort than a place in which to be anxious.

Mr. Downing and Father Fewling meet in the Warden's Shelter one evening towards the close of *Northbridge Rectory*. The two burn their mouths on cocoa and discuss the early courtship of Mr. Downing and Mrs. Turner, without naming her outright (260-61). The Shelter has bunks and little stove and the grown men crouch to be comfortable within. They are both too old for their surroundings and their topic. They are grown men at a watch post in wartime, and one, Father Fewling, has even been in the Navy, but they appear more like boys in a secret tree house gossiping about girls. These middle-aged men in Northbridge are trying to adjust to their disrupted social roles, as they are lumped in with the "women spotters," boys, old men and the disabled, but do not fit into any of these categories. Again, Thirkell is making the point that wartime duties are sometimes ineffective, and in this case, the characters even appear a bit juvenile.

While it may have been optional to obey the sirens and commit to volunteer opportunities, rationing was a reality. Even Mrs. Villars, who is horrified by her treatment at the hands of the rude shop girls and even ruder customers, has to confront the unreliability of ingredients and the unpleasantness of shopping while trying to keep up with the teas, dinners, and parties she feels obligated as the rector's wife to provide in wartime (*Northbridge Rectory* 113-15). In fact, Mrs. Paxon shows that the neighborhood clearly expects Mrs. Villars, being the rector's wife, to open her house to callers, as well as to boarders, as Mrs. Paxon makes a point of refusing sugar with her tea as an act of wartime solidarity, stating "I couldn't take yours; you have so *many* calls on you" (40).

Shopping for groceries at Scatcherd's Stores is an ordeal for the Northbridge residents. Mrs. Villars is warned by

Mrs. Turner on her way to Scatcherd's that they are doing "a bit of war blackmail" there, and Mrs. Villars observes that it seems the war refugees are able to buy everything up, and anyone who complains is told that "there's a war on" (*Northbridge Rectory* 25-26). The proprietor relays that although his business is doing very well financially in wartime, the behavior of his clientele and employees is terrible. At Scatcherd's, there is another example of class struggle, as Mrs. Villars finds herself forced to appeal to an ungracious salesgirl with "blood-red fingernails fringed with black[dirt]" (113). Clearly, Thirkell does not approve of the young woman's style, through which style the reader is lead to believe that the salesgirl is a low class evacuee who is using the war as a reason not to do her job correctly. After being rudely cut off in line at Scatcherd's, Mrs. Villars tries to appeal to the salesgirl, who snubs her. Mrs. Villars is then accused of not knowing that there's a war on (the ongoing excuse for all bad behavior in the novel), and as a result feels "guilty and miserable. She had only asked to have her fair turn and before she knew where she was she was being practically accused of want of patriotism" (114).

Once the women of Northbridge get their groceries, those groceries are never exactly what the women really wanted or needed. The sporadic availability of ingredients and wartime rationing results in a great deal of creative cooking. As the real-life Mrs. Wood recalls, "Housewives during the war were far better cooks than they've been ever since. Can you believe that? We had so little to manage with, we became inventive... We had fantastic swaps" (Terkel 219). While Mrs. Villars herself never boasts of new culinary creations, Miss Pemberton is such a good and innovative cook that her editor urges her to shelve her esoteric writings and publish a wartime recipe cookbook (*Northbridge Rectory* 187, 221).

Altogether, the volunteering, domestic duties, air raids, bomb-shelters, and bizarre meals are only the trappings of daily life in wartime. While they are the main substance of Thirkell's novel, it is the underlying anxiety of the much ignored war that frames the mundane events. At the Villars' New Year's Party, the couple acknowledges the strangeness of civilian wartime behavior. Watching her guests, Mrs. Villars briefly thinks, "how peculiar it was, judging by the almost forgotten pre-war standards, that what people called 'nothing happening' meant going on living in a state of darkness, discomfort, perpetual unconscious anticipation of danger, or in less favored places than Northbridge in actual horrible danger," and her husband makes a similar analysis (241-242).

Predominately, however, in *Northbridge Rectory* the anxieties of the war are put aside, and Mrs. Villars experiences a certain lightheartedness when she weeds her garden or deals with her servants' minor problems (67). Mrs. Villars is embarrassed at herself for being so often happy and content with her life, aware as she is of the war and the struggles and hard work of her countrymen. Despite her awareness that her happiness is perhaps inappropriate, she finds herself feeling genuine delight from time to time, and she is grateful for those times (67-68).

It is her son in the end who firmly puts Mrs. Villars' mind at rest. He arrives home on leave, a happy, restless, normal young man to whom Thirkell jokingly refers by his military title, "the Wing Commander," while he joyfully arranges movie dates with girls, borrows money, brings home dirty laundry, and accidentally breaks furniture and tea cups in his youthful exuberance (314-317). It is only his title and the fact that he has brought rations with him that indicates a war is on. He behaves more like a son home on school break than like a solider, but like everyone else in the story, he does not obsess about the war. Only because he is "the Wing Commander" is his boyish happiness more significant then any of the other characters' denial of the war's burden. His behavior clearly solidifies Thirkell's intention to soften the negativity of a horrible war. Luckily for the reader, her intention ensures an amusing and delightful story.

Works Cited

Terkel, Studs. *The Good War: An Oral History of World War II*.New York: Ballantine Books, 1984.
Thirkell, Angela. *Northbridge Rectory*. New York: Carroll & Graf Publishers, 1991 (orig. 1941).

Contributor

Ashley Minogue earned his B. A. from Connecticut College, where he was a philosophy major, and he is working on his M. B. A. at Baruch College. His previous work includes fundraising positions at the Brooklyn Historical Society, the Staten Island Museum, and the Lyme Academy of Fine Arts. He is currently a Senior Development Officer at the National Academy Museum and School of Fine Arts in New York City.

"A Spirit of Laughter Born Out Of Its Time": The Woman Writer in the War Novels of Angela Thirkell
by
Elisabeth Lenckos

Trailing tortoiseshell hairpins and her impossible son Tony in her wake, exceedingly modest about her prodigious career in the world of the arts and letters: this is how Angela Thirkell's readers fondly remember Mrs. Morland. The loveable, unpretentious novelist appears in many volumes of the Barsetshire series, and is particularly prominent in the early novels and in the war novels *Cheerfulness Breaks In* (1940) and *Miss Bunting* (1945). As one might guess, Mrs. Morland represents a self-portrait of the author – an independent woman who lacks the need to lay claim to any particular kind of literary genius. Nevertheless, Mrs. Morland enjoys her occupation and is even described as hatching literary plots while others go about the more serious business of organizing the war effort during the Second World War (*Cheerfulness Breaks In* 58).

As the above-referenced passage shows, Mrs. Morland considers "having four sons" more of an inspiration than her literary talent and intelligence combined. She readily concedes that her need to support her widowed self and her four sons, to send them to preparatory schools and colleges, as well as to give them allowances, represents the true driving force behind her tales of mystery about Madame Koska and her dressmaking establishment-cum-spy-ring.

To the modern feminist sensitivity, this understatement in regards to what seems to be a long and prosperous career in the literary world, even if it is that of the mystery genre, comes perhaps as a surprise. However, when one looks at the majority of the novels written by women before, during, and after World War II, it becomes evident that Mrs. Morland is by no means the sole example of a self-effacing woman professional in the female narratives of the era. In fact, the modesty (an old-fashioned term itself) exhibited by women vis-à-vis their callings, whether intellectual or domestic, is a dominant trait in many of the works produced by English women in the middle of the twentieth century. An obvious example is that of E. M. Delafield's *Provincial Lady* (1930), a semi-autobiographical novel in diary form that recounts the adventures of a gentlewoman-turned-author. In *The Provincial Lady Goes to London* (1932), the provincial lady has earned sufficient royalties to buy herself a flat in London, but she is weary of the Bloomsbury scene of famous literati and soon pokes fun at the lack of appreciation and affinity she encounters there. In *The Provincial Lady in Wartime* (1940), she records her experiences in a job in the Air Raid Precautions Headquarters, but the diary ceases when she is given a confidential position in the Ministry of Information. Similarly, Mrs. Morland in *Cheerfulness Breaks In* (1940) puts on hold her career as a writer to work as a secretary to Mr. Birkett and to render war-time service.

Neither Thirkell's nor Delafield's protagonists describe their involvement in the war effort as commendable, heroic or even selfless. Rather, the decision to discontinue their former occupation as authors and "to do their bit for the war" is seen as the natural expression of the urgent desire to help their country and its fighting men. However, both authors' accounts of their war work are unreservedly frank in revealing the mishaps, upheavals, and redundancies created by female war volunteerism, and extraordinarily funny when describing their own sense of futility at the abortive attempts to help with the war, other than in their capacity as writers. The sense of humor manifested in Thirkell's and Delafield's war stories thus intimates the coming return to their true profession as recorders of human experience. Writers, so goes the implied message of their narratives, are needed as urgently on the home front as are all other workers, since they bear testimony to life, not only in its glory, but also its ridiculousness, and they call attention to moments when social ideals turn into existential absurdities. Thirkell and Delafield thus stand in the fine tradition of comical and ironical, "stiff-upper-lip" female writing that blossomed in the years during and after the war. Among them, E. M. Delafield's *Provincial Lady in Wartime* (1940) and Angela Thirkell's *Cheerfulness Breaks In* (1940) are particularly notable.

There are, of course, many other representatives of the humorous war-genre. Elizabeth Taylor's, *At Mr. Lippincote's* (1945) features a highly unconventional woman who insists on her individuality even in times of war, as do the heroines of Ngaio Marsh's *A Surfeit of Lampreys* (1941) and Nancy Mitford's *The Pursuit of Love* (1945). These novels also employ the metaphor of the misfit-family to examine the issue of social conformity, convention, and scandal. Similarly, Dodie Smith*'s I Capture the Castle* (1949) is a coming-of-age novel that pokes fun at the reliance on literary models, such as supplied by Jane Austen's novels, in times of crises. Barbara Pym's *So Very Secret* (written 1941, published 1987) represents a parody of wartime spy novels (the kind that Mrs. Morland writes, perhaps) and is set in the literary world of Oxford University. Finally, Marghanita Laski's 1952 comedy of manners, *The Village* describes, much like Thirkell's *Peace Breaks Out* (1947), the problematic readjustment to post-war life in rural Britain.

Women also wrote serious wartime books. Vera Brittain's *England's Hour* (1941) bears vivid eyewitness testimony to the Battle of Britain as fought on the home front. Virginia Woolf's *Between the Acts* (1941) takes place in 1939 and anticipates the disaster to come in the tensions erupting between the occupants of a country house during a village fete. Elizabeth Bowen's *Heat of the Day* (1949) is a wonderfully evocative novel about war-darkened London and the atmosphere of secrecy, conspiracy and distrust that seeps even into the most loving and devoted relationships. Jocelyn Playfair's *A House in the Country* (1944) ostensibly tells the story of a country estate under siege, but in reality ponders the validity of war and the quality of mercy. Marghanita Laski's *Little Boy Lost* (1945) deals with a father's desperate search for his son in war-torn France. The war stories of Mollie Panter-Downes and Elizabeth Bowen, among them "The Demon Lover" and "But Madame," provide further examples of the excellent writing produced by English women during the Second World War.

What all these novels, whether humorous or serious, have in common is that at their center stands a self-confident, clear-thinking, morally probing, professionally and personally independent woman, whose attempt to come to grips with the changed world around her is described as the true battle to be fought. Victory ensues when the reality of war and the fact of isolation are faced squarely, self-reliance wins the day in a world where old ties no longer function as the sole guarantors of safety, and ideological certainties are under attack from the new forces emerging from the social crisis. Thus, Mrs. Morland's clear-eyed understanding of herself as a fair-to-middling, if extremely popular writer, who is motivated by economic necessity as much as by her calling, reflects the mood of the times. In wartime Britain, *Miss Bunting* shows, all professions took second place to those immediately engaged in the fighting and winning of war, and any kind of self-aggrandizement was regarded as ridiculous when it did not have its cause in an association with the war effort.

However, there is another reason for Mrs. Morland's downplaying of her obvious literary talent, as Ruth Adam argues in her study, *A Woman's Place: 1910-75*:

> A woman born at the turn of the century could have lived through two periods when it was her moral duty to devote herself, obsessively, to her children; three when it was her duty to society to neglect them; two when it was right to be seductively feminine; and three when it was a pressing social obligation to be the reverse. (1)

This statement obviously applies to Mrs. Morland's generation. Thus, it can be argued that Mrs. Morland's restraint in matters of self-promotion arises not only directly from the wartime context of the 1940s, but from a deep-seated uncertainty prompted by the changing ideologies about women's roles during the greater part of twentieth-century history. The situation was not improved by the conviction, prevalent in academic and literary-critical circles, that women writers like Mrs. Morland, and their counterparts in real life, Thirkell, Bowen, Taylor, Pym, Mitford and others, were not first-class, but merely "middlebrow" writers. The classification still persists, although modern-day critics, such as Nicola Humble in *The Feminine Middlebrow Novel 1920s to 1950s: Class, Domesticity, Bohemianism*, argue convincingly for a more respectful reappraisal of the middlebrow novel.

In addition, the trope of women's self-effacement had long enjoyed an established tradition in English literature. It dates at least back to the great Jane Austen, who published her first novels anonymously, and to her contemporary Mary Brunton who declared that:

> [to be] suspected of literary airs – to be shunned, as literary women are, by the more pretending of their own sex, and abhorred, as literary women are, by the more pretending of the other! – my dear, I would sooner exhibit as a rope dancer.
> (Anne Katherine Elwood qtd. in Gilbert and Gubar 108)

This quaintly old-fashioned, but decorous attitude seems to persist in Thirkell's protagonists. In a way, this is not surprising, since Thirkell's nostalgic evocation of the Victorian Age and its great novelists and teachers demonstrates her affinity with a period in history that promoted a strict etiquette of humility concerning the author, especially the woman author, and her attitude towards her literary success (this point has been made by several modern literary critics, among them Anthony Harding, in "Felicia Hemans and the Effacement of Woman").

Last, but not least, Thirkell, and her literary double, Mrs. Morland, take a certain pride in the fact that they stand in a somewhat conservative, understated historical-literary tradition that had no affinity with the less bashful, contemporary literary world of Bloomsbury and other modern writers' circles. To show her detachment from what she regarded as the vagaries of intellectual taste, Thirkell in *Miss Bunting* (like Delafield in *The Provincial Lady in London*) proffers an uproarious parody of a review a Bloomsbury critic might have written, despite the fact that her epithet of "pinky," indicating communist sympathies, is somewhat ungenerous. The passage mocks avant garde writing as well as subjects, with its description of Mrs. Morland as representing "the effete snobbery of a capitalist society," in contrast to an obscure and hypocritical writer on unpleasant subjects (with the hilarious name of Gudold Legpul) (*Miss Bunting* 77).

In this context, neither Thirkell's narrator nor her alter ego appear humble, showing instead what a formidable opponent this author could be to critics who were unfavorably inclined towards her fiction. Such pride was, of course, hard won. As Delafield reported in *The Provincial Lady Goes to London*, few writers were admitted into the exclusive cycles of the true *avant garde* (119). Its members made and broke literary reputations, and bore down hard on those of their writing compatriots whom they did not consider their equal in terms of talent, character, and class. For example, in her biography about Elizabeth Bowen, Victoria Glendenning provides an excellent description of the Bloomsbury literary scene and its abhorrence of middle-class culture. Bowen, although well connected in Oxford, enjoyed a friendship with Virginia Woolf, but never belonged to the Bloomsbury circle, since some of its members found her depictions of middle-class life "vulgar" (90-134).

More importantly, the passage from Delafield's *Provincial Lady* illustrates the tension that was becoming quite explicit at the time, between writers who regarded their profession as a "calling" and self-declared dilettantes such as Angela Thirkell, who presented themselves as merely "dabbling" in literature. Thus, the debate shifted to matters of class, with Thirkell siding squarely with the tradition that regarded women's writing as a pastime which might or might not yield an income (in Mrs. Morland's case, it fortunately does), but was not necessarily seen as a serious career.

Be that as it may, Thirkell does take pride, if not in her literary accomplishments, then in her ability to earn money. Thus, it is significant that *Cheerfulness Breaks In* tells the reader that "Mrs Morland ... was pleased to get her advance on royalties and felt that Tony's education and the pocket money of her other boys were safe for the present" (266). This statement reveals that gainful employment, the knowledge not to constitute a burden but rather, to be capable of supporting others, is a source of joy and pleasure to Mrs. Morland. Surely, part of that pleasure must derive from her feeling a sense of self-worth and independence that only come from a woman knowing she is a professional.

Thus, despite her refusal to lay claim to the title of literary genius, Thirkell peoples her novels with women who are gainfully employed, independent, middle-class professionals. Surprisingly, these female protagonists are permitted to preserve their dignity and self-respect despite the wittily withering attacks launched on other, more elevated and better placed female members of Barsetshire society. These dignified women are most notably, Miss Sparling, the headmistress in *The Headmistress* (1943) and Miss Bunting, the governess in *Miss Bunting* (1945). They are working women like Mrs. Morland, who take pride in their occupations and inspire an excess of awe and respect in a society that as a rule judges severely. In the person of

Miss Bunting, these women are shown to be able to move, ever so reluctantly, with the times, while realizing the need for keeping up the traditional values of British society, even if it is to renew itself. Despite this plucky attitude, Miss Bunting is, of course, a symbol for the Old England. Her story, set in the last year of World War II, ends appositely and oddly hilariously with the dying governess' fantastic vision of Hitler's demise at her hands, followed by her own, more peaceful death (*Miss Bunting* 309).

It is no coincidence that in her resounding finale to the final twelve months of World War II, *Miss Bunting*, Thirkell also features more prominently her writing protagonist, Mrs. Morland as well as another best-selling woman author. This is the indomitable Miss Hampton who, with her companion in life and work, Miss Bent, pays a brief visit to deposit a goat named Pelléas for the local "Bring and Buy" sale (286). The reader is told in *Cheerfulness Breaks In* that Miss Hampton's novels differ from those of Mrs. Morland in that they are based on serious research carried out by herself and her partner, and that the novels tend to deal with psychological and sexual studies – modern topics indeed. Promising revelations about the depravity of state institutions and the "psychology of educational establishments," Miss Hampton's work is even more personally and financially rewarding than is Mrs. Morland's, and Miss Hampton's novels are alternatively touted and condemned by the social and intellectual critics in Britain and the United States (*Cheerfulness Breaks In* 262).

The scene represents a very funny, if damning indictment of the way literary fame, or rather notoriety, promotes the sale of books in modern times. However, Thirkell depicts "strong and gentlemanly" Miss Hampton, who shares with

Miss Bent what our more enlightened age would probably call a [barely] closeted lesbian relationship, as a strangely likeable character. Although the author here implicates Miss Hampton as taking part in the ludicrous machinations of the contemporary book market, she also depicts her as a much valued and beloved member of the Southbridge community. Miss Hampton is a good friend to Miss Bent and to those in need of her aid (the evacuated couple Mr. and Mrs. Bissell), and an excellent aunt who generously supports her nephews. What is more, Miss Hampton is an educated woman with none of the arrogance of the intellectual and writer Fritz Gissing, whose behavior is not only most ungentlemanly, but who is unable to attract the reading masses as she does: as always in Thirkell's world, good behavior is a certain indicator of professional and personal merit.

Yet, there is no doubt that Miss Hampton is also a figure of fun. She is prone to somewhat peculiar habits, constantly renaming her dog after places and countries invaded by Nazi Germany and making a daily routine of visiting the Red Lion Pub as if it were a church. With her no-nonsense, yet slightly ludicrous demeanor and severely tailored clothes, she is a modern variety of "the spinster lady," a literary institution dating back to pantomime dames, to the maiden ladies of Elizabeth Gaskell's *Cranford* and of Mary Russell Mitford's *Our Village*. However, Miss Hampton is also reminiscent of Charles Dickens' loving spinster aunts who give all to the families and friends they love and cheerfully suffer the woes of genteel poverty. Therefore, perhaps not so surprisingly, one of the few outbreaks of personal feelings, a small lover's tiff, which Thirkell describes in *Cheerfulness Breaks In* is one that takes place between Miss Hampton and Miss Bent, as the former astounds her friends with the delicacy of her feeling and her devotion to her friend (268). It is also Miss Hampton who raises to Mrs. Morland the delicate subject of human feeling in her gruff, masculine way, suggesting that Mrs. Morland is too sensitive to read Miss Hampton's latest sensational book (*Cheerfulness Breaks In* 262).

Mrs. Morland's surprise at Miss Hampton's condescension towards her shows not only that emotions and inhibitions are rarely discussed in genteel Southbridge, but that Miss Hampton is a veritable "gentleman" of the old-fashioned, even Victorian variety. She obviously considers a true lady as too fragile to be exposed to revelations regarding bad manners or immorality. Moreover, Thirkell implies that Miss Hampton is a sensitive person, who hides a delicate nature under a thin veneer of abruptness. She is therefore not entirely to be seen as ludicrous, since in the course of the narrative she is depicted as being endowed with depths of character and feeling that are rare in the Barsetshire satires.

Miss Hampton is, in fact, one of the few protagonists in *Cheerfulness Breaks In* of whom the reader's opinion truly changes as the story progresses. If she is at first shown as the quintessential bluestocking, masculine, learned, frigid, she is later revealed as loving, caring, and easily hurt, relying on the seemingly more helpless Miss Bent to see her through life's trials and tribulations. Their relationship is thus a touching, if not altogether unfunny parody of a traditional, heterosexual relationship – that of the Bissells, for example – where the apparently stronger partner is disclosed in the end to be the more vulnerable person. Of course, such relationships seldom occur in Thirkell's novels where as a rule, men hold tight the reins of the marriage carriage, and the women follow in docile fashion. This is the reason why it is all the more impressive that Thirkell succeeds in turning topsy-turvy the rules of familial interaction in this case of two spinsters living as a couple.

The dispute between Miss Hampton and Miss Bent also marks one of the moments when the finer light of irony pervades the rigid black-and-whiteness of satire that so often dominates Thirkell's stories. In general, Thirkell identifies her protagonists according to the extreme conventions of the genre – they are either all good or all bad. Thus, young Gissing is gossiped about as a thoroughly rotten apple in an otherwise sweet-smelling barrel. By contrast, Miss Hampton and Miss Bent surprise Southbridge by the success of Miss Hampton's book, by a modesty that rivals that of Mrs. Morland, by their open patriotism, and by their donations to Miss Hampton's nephews, as well as by their tender regard for each other. By being accepted into its exclusive circle, they also demonstrate that Southbridge society can have an open mind about social aberrations when it likes people and may admit them into its midst as a consequence. Miss Hampton coupled with Miss Bent forms a refreshing exception to the Barsetshire rule that frequently consigns all sorts of marginal groups to London, the United States or to internment camps, rather than allowing them to desecrate permanently the homesteads of the peaceful and harmonious countryside.

Ultimately, Miss Hampton represents Thirkell's plea for patience on the part of society for the woman of letters. As is well known, Thirkell and her family had to live on the income from her royalties, and she obviously puts this piece of autobiographical background into her novels in order to defend herself against charges that it was solely ambition that prompted her to write successful novels. In fact, Thirkell's denigration of writing as a profession may have sprung not so much from her fear of societal disapproval of women writers, but from her own aversion to the world of intellectuals and bohemians who openly flaunted their genius, cleverness and mores in public and in their fiction.

Thirkell responds to what she conceives to be their exhibitionism by creating a protagonist who distinguishes herself by her absence and modesty, and only allows Mrs. Morland on occasion to appear more than a few times. In the peacetime novels, Mrs. Morland reverts back to being a rather elusive presence, the beloved and best-selling Barsetshire author whom everyone knows, reveres and wants to meet, but who only emerges from her home for infrequent visits and festive country occasions. Likewise, there are few, if any, sympathetic writers to be found in Thirkell's later novels where the struggle between urban intellectualism and rural common sense usually reduces the combatants to one-sided caricatures of their real selves.

As a warden of wartime morale, Thirkell can be seen as an ideological conservative, her works the obvious product of a literary history that favored the rise of the novel which in turn favored a burgeoning middle-class, as Nancy Armstrong argues in *Desire and Domestic Fiction*. From this point of view, the world of her characters seems confined to the domestic sphere: the quintessential British village-cum-manor house, where courtship and the marriage customs of the country serve to uphold the old order of a gentrified hierarchy. Change, particularly of the industrial variety, is seen with few exceptions as a bad thing. And although it is implied that the new order might rule in faraway places like London, it will not, nor is it ever likely to, be allowed to conquer the pleasant hierarchy of Barsetshire or upset the serenity of its inhabitants.

Barsetshire is thus presented as a pseudo-ageless sanctum that exists apart from the reality of the modern Britain emerging with World War II and after Victory Day.

Although Thirkell clearly attempts to make sense of the losses and deprivations of the war from the British perspective, the true horrors of battle are for the most part only hinted at in her kind of fiction. If to modern sensitivities her narratives seem too accepting of human calamity, it may be said in Thirkell's defense that she wrote her particular kind of fiction with a firm belief in British superior morale and in the hope of focusing and strengthening British resolve. Thirkell elected to write about the war not from the point of view of the battleground, but from that of the domestic front, because that is where her realm of experience lay. In doing so, she showed her readers a way to cope with home life during war-- not in anger, but in humor, by propagating a female kind of bravado or "stiff upper lip."

In doing so, Thirkell also responded to a need for a literature that allowed her female peers living with the daily drudgery of rationing, deportation, bombing, and the ever-present fear of death a way to restore and preserve in the midst of suffering their inner resources of endurance. In her novels, Thirkell provided many models of such attempts at self-repair. In *Marling Hall* for example, the novel opens with young widow Lettice Watson, who has lost her husband at Dunkirk. When Lettice reflects upon the events of past six years and her "very happy marriage" which ended with her husband being killed, she soon admits to herself that "many other women were far worse off" and "that time was dulling her sense of loss" (*Marling Hall* 7). As is evident from this passage, Thirkell promoted a dictum of cool detachment towards any kind of hardship and created in her fiction examples of behavior with which readers could identify and from which they could draw inspiration for their own lives and losses.

Thus, the accusation of ideological conditioning falls flat to a certain extent when one considers that the novels of Thirkell are fashioned from the stuff of social satire. Her world is one turned upside down, with precocious upper-class children acting wiser than their high-born, yet often vapid parents, simple country folk outwitting urban cosmopolitans, and gentle lords and ladies being made martyrs to their tyrant servants. Thirkell reminds readers of Dickens, Trollope, Austen, and characters of the burlesque theatre, as she introduces readers to personalities that are larger than life, exaggerating their traits and actions almost beyond belief.

As Thirkell presents herself in the guise of the absent-minded, perception-lacking novelist Mrs. Morland, she defies smiling skepticism with ever taller stories about impoverished, unworldly lords winning out over astute business men; wily, old-fashioned peasants defeating the egalitarian attempts of a socialist government; and commanding, pompous men winning the hands of beautiful and clever (or not so clever, but kind-hearted) women. Patronage, bestowed consciously or not, is the order of the day, and most members of Barsetshire society, be they servants who are ordered "not to give themselves airs," or women who are told by men not to be fools, seem to fail to notice they are being made the objects of a certain kind of condescension. Hurt feelings, sensitivities, and inner lives are given little room in Thirkell's world, unless they result in a new engagement or a fortunate alliance among the county set, which in turn guarantees that this completely self-sustaining world will not become extinct.

Thirkell's xenophobia and dislike of the "lower orders" when not confined to the servant or peasant class, make many modern readers (this one included) feel uncomfortable. The ways she portrays foreigners, liberal thinkers, and town dwellers sits uneasily with readers today, and one would wish she had tried to do without such blatant, and sometimes banal, generalizations. However, it is important to remember that if Thirkell is a relentless satirist, the last joke is always directed at her own person. This is evident from the reviews that Mrs. Morland receives for her novels in *Cheerfulness Breaks In*, in which the reviews essentially say "Ah, yes, the same old reliable thing" (266).

The actual passage is simply brilliant, as it subverts in advance any attempts at a literary critique that would accuse a writer (here, Mrs. Morland) of repetitiveness, inappropriate levity, and sensationalist stereotyping, since it anticipates them in a few matter-of-fact judgments. In addition, it reveals that the author has a clear understanding of her own limitations and is willing to undercut any pretenses that she might harbor in regard to her literary and intellectual abilities. This effect is borne out by the scene alluded to earlier in the essay when Mrs. Morland ponders the possibility of doing "real war work": Mr. Birkett points out that she has no qualifications and can best serve the war effort by entertaining the public with her writing, and, with a whiff of self-interest, by doing secretarial work for him (58).

Nowadays, one would expect Mrs. Morland to defend herself against Mr. Birkett's patronizing attitude and to protest that her talents should exempt her from working as a secretary. However, this expectation ignores the humor implicit in this scene. The outline of the novel that Mrs. Morland has just hatched demonstrates that despite her immense popularity with her public, highbrow or not (and schoolmasters admit to reading her works), her novels can hardly count as works of the first caliber in terms of "great literature."

"A spirit of laughter born out of its time," Mrs. Brandon's description of her own sense of humor (*The Brandons* 7), thus applies to Thirkell herself, who was already considered old-fashioned when she wrote and published her Barsetshire series around the events of World War II. That she was aware of the fact is shown by her perspicacious self-criticism. Yet one has to admire her bravado, the legendary "stiff upper lip" that holds out against the post-war Britain, with its new social structures, its new literary innovations, its new generation of self-confident writing men and women. Undeterred by these changes, Thirkell kept describing and praising a bygone world that was to her far superior to the modern one. Her outspoken regard for that earlier world, and the stubborn courage with which she defends it, deserves respect, even if readers can no longer fully understand or appreciate her reasons for doing so. Many modern readers may feel that they can do well without her jingoism, her dislike of the working classes and of other marginal groups, and her belief in what is now called "little England." However, the world she depicts with such humorous panache remains, like that of Austen, attractive to an important degree, and readers find attractive the way she tempers her literary ambitions with the decorum of modesty and self-satire. Angela Thirkell's novels are timepieces, but her characters, especially Mrs. Morland, Miss Bunting, Miss Hampton, and their peers, live on in readers' imaginations. There, they stand as symbols of the ways women fought to represent, and to be represented in, the world before the advent of modern feminism made their lives less burdensome.

Works Cited

Adam, Ruth. *A Woman's Place: 1910-1975*. London: Persephone Books, 2002.

Armstrong, Nancy. *Desire and Domestic Fiction: A Political History of the Novel*. Oxford and New York: Oxford University Press, 1987.

Bowen, Elizabeth. "But, Madame, " 1941 (*The Collected Stories of Elizabeth Bowen*, ed. Angus Wilson. New York: Knopf, 1981.

Bowen, Elizabeth. "The Demon Lover," 1941 (*The Collected Stories of Elizabeth Bowen*, ed. Angus Wilson. New York: Knopf, 1981.

Bowen, Elizabeth. *The Heat of the Day*. Harmondsworth: Penguin, 1962 [orig. 1949].

Brittain, Vera. *England's Hour*. Pleasantville, NY: The Akadine Press, 2002 [orig. 1941].

Delafield, E. M. *The Provincial Lady*. London: Virago, 1991 [orig. 1930]. Collected with other Provincial Lady" novels in the sequence as *The Diary of a Provincial Lady*.

Delafield, E. M. *The Provincial Lady Goes to London*. London: Virago, 1991 [orig. 1932]. Collected with other "Provincial Lady" novels in the sequence as *The Diary of a Provincial Lady*.

Delafield, E. M. *The Provincial Lady in Wartime*. London: Virago, 1991 [orig. 1940]. Collected with other "Provincial Lady" novels in the sequence as *The Diary of a Provincial Lady*.

Gaskell, Elizabeth, *Cranford*, 1853.

Gilbert, Sandra M. and Susan Gubar. *The Madwoman in the Attic: The Woman Writer and the Nineteenth-Century Literary Imagination*. New Haven and London: Yale University Press, 1979.

Glendenning, Victoria. *Elizabeth Bowen: A Biography*. New York: Knopf, 1977.

Harding, Anthony. "Felicia Hemans and the Effacement of Woman," *Romantic Women Writers: Voices and Countervoices*, ed. Paula R. Feldman and Theresa M. Kelley. Hanover: University Press of New England, 1995.

Humble, Nicola. *The Feminine Middlebrow Novel 1920s to 1950s: Class, Domesticity, Bohemianism*. Oxford: Oxford University Press, 2001.

Laski, Marghanita. *Little Boy Lost*. London: Persephone Books, 2001 [orig. 1945].

Laski, Marghanita. *The Village*. London: Persephone Books, 2004 [orig. 1952].

Marsh, Ngaio. *A Surfeit of Lampreys*. Harmondsworth: Penguin, 1959 [orig. 1941].

Mitford, Mary Russell. *Our Village*, 1843.

Mitford, Nancy. *The Pursuit of Love*. Harmondsworth: Penguin, 1945.

Playfair, Joyce. *A House in the Country*. London: Persephone Books, 2003 [orig. 1944].

Pym, Barbara. *So Very Secret*. Published first in: *Civil to Strangers and Other Writings*, ed. Hazel Holt, New York: E.P. Dutton, 1987 [written in 1941].

Smith, Dodie. *I Capture the Castle*. London: Reprint Society 1950 [orig. 1949].

Taylor, Elizabeth. *At Mrs. Lippincote's*. London: Virago, 1995 [orig. 1945].

Thirkell, Angela. *Cheerfulness Breaks In*. New York: Carroll & Graff, 1996 [orig. 1940].

Thirkell, Angela. *The Brandons*. New York: Carroll & Graff, 1996 [orig. 1939].

Thirkell, Angela. *The Headmistress*. Wakefield, Rhode Island and London: Moyer Bell, 1996 [orig. 1943].

Thirkell, Angela. *Marling Hall*. New York: Carroll & Graf, 1995 [orig. 1942].

Thirkell, Angela. *Miss Bunting*. Wakefield, Rhode Island and London: Moyer Bell, 1996 [orig. 1945].

Thirkell, Angela. *Peace Breaks Out*. Wakefield, Rhode Island and London: Moyer Bell, 1997 [orig. 1947].

Woolf, Virginia *Between the Acts*. London: Harcourt, 1941.

Contributor

Elisabeth Lenckos was educated at Bonn University in Germany, the University of Salamanca in Spain, and the University of Sussex in Great Britain. She holds an M. A. from Indiana University and a Ph. D. in Comparative Literature from the University of Michigan. She is the editor of *All This Reading: The World of Barbara Pym*, and she has published articles on Victorian and modern women's poetry and prose in various journals. She teaches in the Graham School at the University of Chicago and leads seminars at the Newberry Library there. She is active in the Jane Austen Society and the Barbara Pym Society and is an associate of the Longfellow Institute at Harvard University. She is currently at work on two books: *Jane Austen and the Modern Writer* and *The Wartime Writings of Twentieth-Century British Women*.

Thirkell Themes in
Peace Breaks Out
by
Kim Hendrickson Leffler

Peace Breaks Out is a 'typical' Angela Thirkell novel –
with three romances, even more if one counts Sylvia
Halliday's and Anne Fielding's crushes on David Leslie.
By the end of the book Sylvia, the golden 'Winged
Victory' (72, 105-06), has come to her senses and become
engaged to Martin Leslie, Anne Fielding has come to *her*
senses and become engaged to Robin Dale, her best friend,
and David, who really is the "bone-selfish" creature his
father often describes, and has never cared anything for
either Sylvia or Anne beyond a mild flirtation to assuage
his boredom, has become engaged to his cousin, Rose
Bingham, who will easily meet his requirement that his true
love be 'funny as hell all the time' (162). Sadly, the book's
last paragraph describes the long-expected death of Dr.
Dale, but not before he has learned of, and approved of,
Robin and Anne's engagement. For those keeping track, it
is in *Peace Breaks Out* that David first comments on 14-
year old Clarissa's 'tip-tilted' fingers (86).

Peace Breaks Out also has the requisite tea parties, Sales of
Work, and Bring and Buy Sales, which occur with
comforting regularity, war or peace notwithstanding. But
things have most definitely changed in Barsetshire since
War Broke Out, and now, when Peace Breaks Out, the
reader begins to see the effects. A closer look at the book
reveals the real emotions and concerns felt by the

characters on many levels. One would think that the end of six years of privation, hardship, and fear would engender a joyous response in the inhabitants of Barsetshire, but one would be wrong. In fact, the onset of peace produces a curious mixture of apprehension and resentment, with various characters resisting the change to peace, just as they have adapted to the exigencies of war. George Halliday points out that peace will bar him getting his promotion, and David Leslie shows his uncertainty about what he should do with his own future (72-73). Thirkell makes ironic reference to the young people being trepidatious about "the dangers and horrors of peace," despite them having dealt with the much greater dangers and horrors of war (73).

As the prospect of peace becomes an increasing reality, a number of the characters in the book begin to realize exactly what the war has meant to them, and how much of their lives have been committed to it or affected by it. Sylvia Halliday, for instance, has spent time in the W.A.A.F. , but, because of the lost years of war, has missed her opportunity to be a dancer (4). She mentions, to David Leslie's shock, that at age twenty-two, she has never been abroad (because of the war) (187). This type of cultural deprivation is mentioned time and again. Many of Barsetshire's children have never known anything but war. People like David sadly recognize that even when peace does come, nothing ever will be the same: David may be selfish, but he is also bright, and he reflects that old people are unwanted, middle-aged people under too much strain, and young people having very little fun, except for the few, like Frances Harvey and Dame Monica Hopkinson, who thrive on bossing others (67). He also regrets the mingling with the uncultured classes (English speaking ballet, uncomfortably crowded with men with wild hair, and women with bare legs, everyone smoking!) that must inevitably result (103).

Similarly, Lady Fielding worries about the impending peace, but reconciles herself to it, there being no other choice. However, she remembers the joys and pleasures of life before the war, and wishes with all her heart that something close to it could be restored. In a lyrical passage describing the mundane activities and movements of people in the Cathedral Close, Lady Fielding harks back to the past and enjoys for a few moments the illusion that war, and the subsequent "pinchbeck" peace, have never happened (142-43).

Nevertheless, peace is looming on the horizon, and while the universal response of Thirkell's characters is dismay, there are some possible advantages to a ceasefire. With her usual sardonic wit, Thirkell presents some of her characters talking about the possible peace and notes that "all the arguments were based on complete ignorance or fine crusted prejudice," as exemplified by Mr. Birkett's idiosyncratic remarks that his two requirements for peace are that England should get Calais back and that there should be more butter available (50-51). Sir Robert (Fielding) joins in with an unsentimental suggestion that ungrateful children should be forced to give up their rations to the grown-ups, and Robin Dale supports him, noting that oranges are spoiling because they are supposed to be available only to children, but that he sees children cynically selling unwanted oranges outside the Odeon (51).

One of the most entertaining, and typically Thirkell-ish, parts of *Peace Breaks Out* is Thirkell's description of the means by which the residents of Hatch End, the village in which the Hallidays live, learn about the impending announcement of peace. Mrs. Hubback, the shopkeeper, warns George Halliday to tell his mother to lay in bread, indicating that the shops will be closed for the peace (122).

Anne Fielding winkles out the information from George and Sylvia that Mrs. Hubback's remarks refer to peace, but Anne is at sea about their reaction. George notes that the impending day of celebration will interrupt his plans to go to London, while Sylvia regrets that now her promotion will not occur (123). While Anne is awed by the prospect of peace, George and Sylvia are so beaten down by the war that they cannot express much joy at its end. Indeed, perhaps because it had been apparent for several months that the war was winding to an end, so the peace came as an anticlimax for some, Thirkell remarks that "'On the following Tuesday a day of national rejoicing burst by very slow degrees and barely recognized as such upon an exhausted, cross and uninterested world" (*Peace Breaks Out* 131-32).

Another interesting aspect of the book, and one reason peace is not welcomed unreservedly by Thirkell's characters, is the subtext concerning the social orders. Chauffeurs, maids, and other household help have joined the war effort and will not likely return to their service positions; evacuees from the city with whom county residents would never ordinarily have associated have become social equals; and others, intensely disliked, such as the Harveys, have attained positions of authority. The future does not look promising for a restoration of the comfortable understanding of societal roles, most of which are presented as having been quite acceptable to all concerned, certainly to the class with which Thirkell is concerned. In a few cases the war has provided an opportunity for different classes to learn more about, and possibly appreciate, each other. At first accepted with a grudging sense of duty, for instance, the Hosiers' Boys' School personnel have become a respected part of the community. Miss Hampton says that "she could have made something of [the Hosiers' teachers]" if they had stayed a bit longer (56-57), and Mr. Birkett concedes that Mr. Bissell, the Hosiers' Headmaster, "was one of the most upright, unselfish characters he had ever met," but is forced to admit, in response to Sir Robert Fielding's questioning, that they did not change each other's outlook at all (54-55).

Mr. Scatcherd, the local artist, personifies the struggle for balance in the Brave New World. As an artist, he would like to feel that he is on the same social plane as the Hallidays and Lady Graham, but he can't help being obsequious, and despises himself for doing so, all the while fearing to act above himself (17-27, 67-69, 87-89). Fortunately, Southbridge School maintains an even keel. Boys and Masters know exactly what their roles are, and relish the comfort of tradition. The scene in Robin Dale's room on Sports Day exemplifies this tradition: Frank Gresham takes a sort of pleasure in silently scuffling for position with Leslies Major and Minor until Robin remembers to announce that it is Open Season in his room, which gives permission for a prep school boy actually to speak to Upper School boys, and for them to notice the existence of a younger boy (176).

This tea party is the occasion of the comeuppance of the odious Miss Banks by Leslie Major, who in a "voice of angelic innocence" asks Robin if he would play Holst's *Uranus* for them one day (182). Later that evening Leslie Major seals Miss Banks' fate by pronouncing *Uranus*, to the shock of Mr. Birkett, as *Uraynus*, which, he explains, is "how Miss Banks pronounces it, and as she is awfully keen on modern methods I thought perhaps Mr. Dale had taught us all wrong" (185). In the terrifying silence that follows, the adults reconsider the proposition that Leslie Major is uncommonly dull, and Miss Banks' position as Latin Master for the lower school is suddenly in jeopardy. Her departure will go a long way to restoring the pre-war composition of the teaching staff.

Other aspects of the dreaded peace will not be as beneficial. Life has changed forever in Barsetshire. At least with the war one knew where one was. On VJ Day Mrs. Morland expresses the thought on everyone's mind, when she suggests all the lovely elements of the past are gone, wiped out by the war, but " 'Don't be a fool, Laura,' said Lord Stoke. . . . 'World's got to go on somehow' " (304). Lady Graham ably seconds him:

> "Yes, it is all *dreadful*," said Lady Graham sympathetically. "But you will write another book, Mrs. Morland, won't you, and we shall all read it aloud, shan't we Clarissa darling, with Gran and Merry."
>
> (305)

Lord Stoke and artless Lady Graham have put it perfectly. Unsettling peace notwithstanding, life will go on, and books will be written and enjoyed, especially those by Angela Thirkell.

Works Cited

Thirkell, Angela. *Peace Breaks Out*. Wakefield, RI: Moyer Bell, 1997 [orig. 1946].

Contributor

Kim Leffler majored in English Literature at Oakland University. She first learned about Angela Thirkell while reading Betty MacDonald's *Onions in the Stew* and knew that any favorite author of a favorite author would be a favorite of hers, too. She joined the Angela Thirkell Society in 1999. English writers top her reading lists, and one of her prize possessions is a handwritten response from P.G. Wodehouse to a fan letter she wrote to him in 1970. She has just published her first book, *HealthWatch Personal Medical Record and Disease Prevention Guide*, and is working on two more manuscripts.

Thinking Again about Geoffrey Harvey
by
Penelope Fritzer

Perspective is paramount to anyone engaged in making judgments, so it is interesting to examine from a different perspective a character who is not quite what he appears to be at first blush. Geoffrey Harvey is introduced in *Marling Hall*, where he is presented as a self-involved and effete aesthete: Cynthia Snowden says that he "brought a taste of Bloomsbury to Barsetshire—and it was a taste which nobody liked" (40). This is the only book in which Geoffrey Harvey is a main character, although he does play an ongoing but lesser role in *The Duke's Daughter*, where he is Tom Grantly's boss. In several other books, Geoffrey makes minor appearances or scornful reference is made to him, the various characters recalling his behavior and his sister with equal repugnance.

There are several notable aspects of Geoffrey Harvey that must be examined in order to get a clear picture of him as a character. Those aspects include his class, his appearance, his accomplishments, and, most importantly, his manners (speech and behavior toward his friends, their parents, his landlady, his ex-governess, the Marlings' governess, the Mixo-Lydian Ambassadress, and his sister Frances). Geoffrey Harvey has many admirable traits that clearly show him, despite the opinion of the other characters, to be gentle, polite, agreeable, and intelligent.

CLASS:

The Harveys, brother Geoffrey and sister Frances, are clearly of the "right" class. They mingle well with the upper and upper middle class characters of Barsetshire, and Geoffrey, like most Barsetshire men, has been to university. Barbara Burrell writes that although he has supposedly been to Cambridge, his college, Lazarus, is actually part of Oxford (190). It is doubtful that Thirkell, whose father was an academic, would make this kind of error, so Geoffrey's university experience is probably a deliberate evocation of "Oxbridge," conflating the traditional English university experience.

More surprising because she is female, Frances Harvey has also been to an unnamed university, one where she took a first in economics (*Marling Hall* 262), quite an accomplishment for a woman of her time and reminiscent of the academic career of Winifred Tebben described throughout *August Folly*. Frances Harvey is presented as rather an unpleasant character, a view certainly in line with Thirkell's well-known feelings about educated women, so it is important to note in light of those feelings that Frances, despite her first in a very difficult subject, did not take an "acceptable" degree, since Thirkell indicates in several places throughout the Barsetshire oeuvre that "modern" topics are not nearly as respectable as is study of the ancients.

The Harveys show their "rightness" in that they have the same upper middle class aesthetic taste as most of their Barsetshire peers: Geoffrey and David Leslie are quite funny about the Red House which is so campy with its fake "this," substitute "that," and imitation "other" (*Marling Hall* 57-62). David says that he is embarrassed by his relatives recommending such a house, and Geoffrey avers that the cement dwarves are a special attraction (58-59), all of this comic chat, of course, in the context of a severe housing shortage during the war, so that the Harveys are desperate to get the house, despite their view of its decoration.

The Harveys also show they are at ease in the social milieu in which they move and have moved. They are cousins of Lady Norton (who is herself a cousin of Mr. Marling) (43), and as young people they have had a French governess and as adults have a faithful retainer former nurse who is now their cook and who must be accommodated as they look for a rental (44). Geoffrey Harvey knows David Leslie socially from London, and Geoffrey is clearly an appropriate friend for Oliver Marling. Geoffrey also knows Julian Rivers, another artistic type, whom Geoffrey (unwittingly in alignment with Barsetshire thinking) considers "conceited," and whose father is a relation of Lord Pomfret (49).

Additionally, Geoffrey later frequents the County Club (*The Duke's Daughter* 27), to which the socially acceptable must be elected (*Love Among the Ruins* 3). The Harveys are definitely the "right" people of the "right" class, so their class is not the reason for them being despised: rather, despite the fact that they are the "right" people, for other reasons they fill a role somewhat like of the Bishop of Barchester, in that most of the characters unite to dislike them, with that dislike increasing as time passes and they are mere references in later books. In fact, when Mr. Marling suggests in *The Duke's Daughter* that he thought his daughter Lucy had at one time been interested in Geoffrey Harvey, she replies "I'd as soon have married the bishop. How *could* you, father?" (45).

APPEARANCE:

Both the Harveys are quite good looking (despite later recurrent descriptions of Frances as looking "hard"). Frances is described as a "very handsome girl" with "fine eyes" (*Marling Hall* 89-90), while Geoffrey is a "tall, lean man with dark eyes and a great deal of dark hair, which was perpetually falling over one eye and as often being thrown back by a toss of his head or put aside by one of his long and very well-shaped hands" (41-42). He is clearly much better looking than is Oliver Marling with his bony, balding head (*Love Among the Ruins* 268) or even David Leslie with *his* bony, balding head (*Peace Breaks Out* 259, 264, 271), two other comparably tall, sophisticated men whose lives are similarly oriented toward London. David clearly does not care for Geoffrey, and often seems quite petty toward him: even when Geoffrey leans down to David's car to speak with him, David says spitefully "The worst of a little car like mine is that if you bend down to talk to anyone inside it you look so peculiar from behind," whereupon "Mr. Harvey straightened himself with a slightly hurried negligence" (*Marling Hall* 58), but does not make even a mild rejoinder.

Geoffrey's occasional posturing, along with Thirkell's emphasis on his long hair, his "well-shaped hands," and his friend Peter, leads to the speculation that he is gay or bisexual. Indeed, he is definitely attracted to the "quiet elegance and the reserved though perfectly cordial manners" of both Oliver Marling and Lettice Watson (49).

There occasionally seems a slightly ominous overtone in David Leslie's assertions about knowing Geoffrey in town, perhaps giving one to wonder how David knows so much about Geoffrey's social life and why he seems so jealous of him. David's petulance, remarks about personal appearance, and grasp of social subtleties is also quite unusual in Barsetshire males, as is his quick boredom and flitting from female to female with no real interest in any of them. Even his proposal to Lettice Watson seems to be wrenched out of him, from some inner idea that marriage would be good for him, and Rose Bingham, the wife he finally marries at her command, when neither of them is still young, is a sophisticate with something of the dominatrix about her (*Peace Breaks Out* 244).

In the end, Geoffrey finds them all somewhat dull and really seems to be attached to his life in London, where he is also an acquaintance of Lionel Harvest (89), who seems pretty clearly gay in *Wild Strawberries*: Lionel enters into a "companionate marriage" with Joan Stevenson after she discovers he is in line for a big inheritance from his father the general (*Wild Strawberries* 236, 254-55). Frances makes what could be read as insinuating reference to Peter and "all his rotten little friends," but, in fact, Peter has apparently extended his wartime invitation to share his flat to Frances as well as to Geoffrey (*Marling Hall* 267).

ACCOMPLISHMENTS:

Even before Geoffrey Harvey's first appearance, Mary Leslie repeats an admittedly liberal opinion that Geoffrey has given about the Russians [England's allies during the war], leading David Leslie to refer to him as "a long-haired member of the intelligentsia talking hot air" and says that he's known Geoffrey around town for some time (37). David, however, dismissive he is about Geoffrey, has not himself been able to actually publish anything beyond an early novel nor to hold a job until after the war, despite his rather languid efforts in both directions in *Wild*

Strawberries.   Geoffrey, by contrast, has made solid progress in both his Civil Service career, where he works with David's brother John Leslie, and in his literary efforts (his publisher is Johns and Fairfield).

Oliver Marling is, like Geoffrey Harvey, quite intellectual, but he is far more pompous about his meager accomplishments: in *County Chronicle* Oliver has written a monograph about Thomas Bohun, Canon of Barchester, that is not long enough to be even privately printed as a book, and he talks on and on about it to Isabel Dale. By contrast, Geoffrey is a published author with a novel about Pico della Mirandola and several poems to his credit, and he is supposedly working on a study of Jehan le Capet (Snowdon 40-41), the same poet who so engaged Hilary Grant (*The Brandons* 97).

Geoffrey Harvey was "bombed out of London in the last blitz," so has come to Barsetshire, where his government office, the Board of Red Tape and Sealing Wax, satirically named but apparently important to the war effort, has moved (*Marling Hall* 42). Although Geoffrey is in England throughout the war, he has a social conscience: he reflects to himself that "at least he was not an able-bodied young man who had found a non-combatant job. He was well over military age. . . ." (49). He is also quite accomplished at his job, a quality admitted by other characters, even as they malign him, and one recognized by Geoffrey himself, who had expected to be made a Knight of the British Empire until the disruption of the war (50). Geoffrey has previously been to France with the Red Cross in 1939 (*The Duke's Daughter* 39), and has even been decorated by the French for talks given behind the Maginot Line (194). Geoffrey is, in fact, so good at his job that his friend Peter calls to say that Geoffrey's old boss has offered to get him released from his Barsetshire job because he is needed in London (*Marling Hall* 266).

Twelve years later, the Harveys are foisted upon Sir Robert Fielding for the night. When Sir Robert brings them to the Deanery to visit, the Dean's expression is "far from hospitable," even while he tells the group that Geoffrey Harvey "did his work [during the war and after] . . . extremely well" (*What Did It Mean?* 248-49). Similarly, in *Love Among the Ruins* the Birketts relate with pleasure that the incompetent Miss Banks had a row with Geoffrey Harvey and he fired her when they were both working for the Pan European Union for General Interference, which would seem to indicate that he is a good administrator who recognizes lackluster employees (19).

The most problematic aspect of Geoffrey Harvey comes not in *Marling Hall* (in which he is really quite charming and tries hard to make himself agreeable and to please everyone from the Marlings to his sister to the boss who requests that he return to London), but rather some years later in *The Duke's Daughter*, in which Thirkell clearly casts him as a villain for his supposedly harsh treatment of Tom Grantly. Looked at dispassionately, Geoffrey Harvey meets Tom at the County Club and gets him a temporary job without him having to take a Civil Service exam; if Tom works out, eventually he can be made permanent (*The Duke's Daughter* 27). Tom begins his position with "a quite unaccountable sick and sinking feeling in his heart," so that the reader who knows Geoffrey Harvey's reputation as an excellent administrator may not be surprised that he recognizes Tom's ambivalence and lack of commitment (*The Duke's Daughter* 54).

Geoffrey takes Tom along to evaluate The Lodge as possible office space, but as the Harveys discuss admittedly horrible ways to reconfigure the space, Tom wanders off and visits with Lady Cora Waring, instead of concentrating on the task at hand (94-99). Tom goes back often to Rushwater, and "although he still hoped that in time some usefulness might come out of what he was doing, he thought of Rushwater a great deal" (120). Concomitantly, Agnes Graham reports, rather ominously from her husband, that Geoffrey "has a name for breaking his underlings if he doesn't like them" (137). Why he might be kind enough to hire Tom and then want to get rid of him on a whim is never explained, so, given Tom's conflicted feelings about his job, and the fact that his interests clearly lie elsewhere, one might surmise that Geoffrey Harvey could possibly prefer a more committed and enthusiastic employee for any permanent position.

Throughout *The Duke's Daughter*, Tom complains about Geoffrey, apparently feeling neither gratitude nor loyalty for Geoffrey having hired him, given the very tight job market and competition among returning veterans for decent jobs. Various characters, beginning with his parents, indicate to Tom from time to time that they think he is wasting his time in a bureaucratic job and that he would be much better off at Rushwater, but no one quite explains why a future as an agricultural laborer is so advantageous. Indeed, if Tom did not eventually marry Emmy Graham (who comes with a job on an estate and a life interest in a very nice house, courtesy of her cousin Martin Leslie), his farming fate would be quite uncertain.

Agnes Graham makes another contribution, remarking that although she has never met Mr. Harvey, Mrs. Marling tells her "he is quite dreadful and unscrupulous" (*The Duke's*

Daughter 167), certainly not behaviors apparent from Mrs. Marling's exposure to Geoffrey in *Marling Hall*. Similarly, Lord Lufton says "That man Harvey . . . has a name for being unfair to his people if they are ladies or gentlemen or interested in anything but getting on," seemingly a clear indication that Geoffrey (himself a gentleman with no reason to be rude to his peers) expects dedication rather than dilettantism (*The Duke's Daughter* 178). One of the few characters who tries to keep an open mind about Geoffrey Harvey is Cecil Waring, who says of Tom that "apparently he has been getting across his chief . . ." and in response to Leslie Waring Winter's remark that Geoffrey only got a measly B. E. and thinks he is important, "Come, come, be fair. Some people are important" (188), although in another instance he says of Geoffrey, "Harvey is intolerable" (100).

MANNERS:

Geoffrey Harvey has a certain complacency in *Marling Hall*, but he never brags, and he keeps both his thoughts and his ambitions to himself. Certainly, his interior monologues, funny though Thirkell makes them, as in his rumination at a dinner party (281-82) or his thoughts on returning to London (299-300), are no more self-involved than those of many Barsetshire characters (and not nearly as unkind as those of David Leslie), and he shows greater patience and restraint than do most.

Despite the way Thirkell presents Geoffrey Harvey, filtered through the eyes of the Barsetshire characters, she also points out that he has his advocates, particularly in regards to his habit of tossing back his hair, which makes him seem "so innocent and defenseless that he could not even protect himself against his own hair," a quality that at least some of his [presumably London] friends find charming, but which makes others dislike him even more (*Marling Hall* 41- 42). Thirkell's wisdom as a writer means that truth will out: in *Marling Hall* Geoffrey actually IS quite innocent and defenseless with everyone with whom he comes in contact.

In all regards, Geoffrey is amazingly polite. He is particularly tolerant of Mr. Marling's quirks: Geoffrey tolerates being repeatedly called "Carver," never correcting his host, and when Geoffrey refuses a second glass of port and his host pours it anyway, Geoffrey obediently drinks it down, albeit quickly, earning from Mr. Marling nothing but dislike for his efforts (*Marling Hall* 286-87).

Geoffrey is also very polite to his hostess. In a rather unattractive show of her hospitality, or lack thereof, Mrs. Marling asks him a conventional question "in a voice which accurately conveyed to her son and daughter exactly what she thought of him," which opinion is recognized by Lettice and Oliver, who "wondered if Geoffrey Harvey would be quick enough to spot it" (42), rather deep waters for an unsuspecting guest invited for a simple drink. Mrs. Marling's dislike is a bit puzzling, since she has never met Mr. Harvey before, but it apparently stems from his hair, since she prefers better groomed men (*Marling Hall* 45); although Oliver has long hair, he keeps it brushed back (44).

To none of these undertones does Geoffrey Harvey respond, only replying in a self-effacing manner to their interest in his job of dealing with "dull and mostly useless correspondence and putting people off who want to know things" (43). Mrs. Marling makes an obscure reference "testing her man," which test he lives up to by recognizing the reference, so she goes for him yet again, asking about his cousins, and when Geoffrey starts to reply, again with a deprecating remark, catches him up by noting that the cousin in question, Victoria Norton, is a relation, causing Geoffrey to apologize (43). Finally, Mrs. Marling relents and joins in bashing Lady Norton (43), and later proving helpful in the matter of the Red House. Geoffrey further shows his agreeable nature when Mrs. Marling asks what kind of house he wants to rent and he replies " 'The dream house of course,' . . . mocking himself a trifle obviously" to which Oliver makes a joke, and Geoffrey, "who liked showing people that he appreciated their remarks, laughed again" (*Marling Hall* 44).

Later, when Mr. Marling, in a rage about waiting an hour for Oliver and having to listen to George Norton's views on agriculture, meets Geoffrey for the first time and persistently calls him "Carver", in addition to being quite insulting about the Nortons, Geoffrey's cousins, Geoffrey quickly tries to put him at ease with a little joke (47). The Harvey/Carver business goes on throughout this book and beyond, but Geoffrey is unfailing polite and patient with Mr. Marling (*Marling Hall* 92), whose dislike of Geoffrey, like Mrs. Marling's, is apparently based on Geoffrey's haircut (80), and who refers to him in another book as a "poisonous feller," scoffing at his Red Cross work (*The Duke's Daughter* 41).

Geoffrey notices how much Lucy Marling is like her father, in her bossiness and her perfect self-confidence, and he far prefers the elegance and reserve of Oliver and Lettice (*Marling Hall* 48-49). By the time of *The Duke's Daughter*, Mrs. Marling is back to snubbing Geoffrey, even as he compliments her on her coffee, since her view of him is so biased that his "diplomatic laugh . . . sounded to Mrs. Marling like a nasty, spiteful giggle" (42).

Geoffrey Harvey is even worse at protecting himself from Joyce Smith, his landlady at the Red House, and from Mademoiselle Duchaux, the Harveys' former governess. It is in his interactions with these two that his true gentleness and good manners show to their best advantage. It would be very easy for him to treat either of them dismissively, as both are female and beneath him in class, and neither is in a position of importance. Joyce Smith, once the lease is signed, derives her power only from her tenants' reluctance to be firm in the face of her depredations for fear of hurting her feelings, even though they are paying her a substantial rent for the use of her supposedly fully furnished house.

From the very beginning of her interactions with him, Joyce Smith creates in Geoffrey a tremendous feeling of guilt: she constantly pleads her widowhood while denuding the house of its small furnishings, as he shows enormous forbearance, controlling himself even as she handles his books which "were to him like parent, child, and wife" (*Marling Hall* 75). Geoffrey wishes he and his sister had stayed at Norton Park where they would be apart from some of the sort of invasions that Joyce Smith and others make, and he contemplates changing the locks as he fends off Lucy Marling's philistine remarks about literature (76-79).

Mademoiselle Duchaux, their former governess, comes every year to visit the Harveys, and they find her quite hard to take. Lettice Watson very graciously invites Mademoiselle Duchaux's nephew to tea, as the Harveys have another engagement and are at their wits' end having entertained Mlle. Duchaux, let alone her nephew, since both are very trying with their constant criticism of all things English (289). But despite what the other characters think of the Harveys, they have a sense of noblesse oblige to their old governess, and would not think of turning her or her nephew away. Even in the face of the great emotional upheaval of his argument with his sister over breaking the lease, Geoffrey rallies himself to offer sherry to the soldiers of color who drop off Mlle. Duchaux's nephew, a nice contrast to Lucy Marling's comments (*Marling Hall* 307).

Similarly, Geoffrey is very polite to Miss Bunting, the governess he meets through the Marlings, even though she is quite firm with him, questioning him relentlessly and making him feel inadequate about his schooling, his civil service work, his social life and his writing (83-84). Geoffrey, by contrast, is meticulously polite, far more so than she, typical of his interaction with most of the other characters. Since politeness and restraint are such major elements in middle and upper middle class behavior, it is interesting that many of the "acceptable" characters feel it is quite all right to snub Geoffrey for his attempts at agreeable remarks and mild jokes.

Even Frances Harvey is a sympathetic character in regard to Joyce Smith and Mademoiselle Duchaux: like her brother, she will not be rude to, or even firm with, them. Indeed, her only real crime in *Marling Hall* is to want to marry someone to whom she is attracted, a position in which almost every Barsetshire heroine finds herself sympathetically portrayed, but one that brings the author's derision on Frances. When it comes to Barsetshire, the Harveys can't win for losing, and it is almost as big a relief to the reader sympathetic to Geoffrey, as it clearly is to him, when he packs up and goes back to London.

Geoffrey not only doesn't defend himself against David Leslie, the Marling parents, Joyce Smith, and the governesses, but he cannot stand up to his sister Frances at all. She is the older sibling and the bossier, and she gets the better of Geoffrey in nearly all their exchanges, because he is so reluctant make a scene. Aside from his argument with Frances about leaving the Red House, the rare instance of Geoffrey losing patience in *Marling Hall* comes when Frances replies to David's goading, saying she is just trying to prove the absurdity of a particular argument, to which her brother responds disloyally but mildly "And so you did" (*Marling Hall* 284).

At his old boss's offer to bring him back to London, Geoffrey shows his true colors as kind, thoughtful, and loyal: although London is his heart's desire, Geoffrey's response is to ask what about his sister, to which Sir Edward replies that he will make an effort for her as well (266). Geoffrey is very excited about going back to London, to the extent that he says, showing his real feelings, "My God, Frances, we may be out of this damned hole by the New Year" (266). Frances' response is to remind him they have a lease and to point out that they have nowhere to live in London, to which Geoffrey replies that his friend Peter has invited both of them to live in his flat, but Frances says, ungratefully, "With how many other people? All his rotten little friends in and out, night and day. . . . you are frightfully selfish, Geoffrey" (267). The reader perhaps is wondering by this point why Geoffrey is reluctant to leave her in Barsetshire.

Time and again, Frances prevails in their interactions, until, desperate and cornered, Geoffrey arranges to give the Red House back to Joyce Smith. He decides near the end *Marling Hall* that it is worth one terrible scene with

Frances, although he fears that she may kill him, in order to break their lease and get out of Barsetshire (302-03). Thirkell is extremely funny about their discussion: although during their argument Geoffrey is terrified, he reminds himself that Frances "had not got a gun or a sword [so] he valiantly stood his ground" (*Marling Hall* 305).

Several years later, in *The Duke's Daughter*, the Harveys are looking at The Lodge with Cecil Waring, with an eye to renting it for government use, since Geoffrey's office has been decentralized and part of it moved to Barsetshire. Frances Harvey keeps suggesting partitions, and her brother finally jokingly says, in one of his few instances of even mild recrimination, "I do wish, Frances, that you would stop being so partition-minded. It's as bad as the partition of Poland," whereupon she crushes him with "Cheap humour won't get you anywhere, Geoffrey" (99).

After Geoffrey has hired Tom Grantly for the office, several of the characters meet in Babs' Buttery for lunch. When Geoffrey sees them, he greets everyone nicely and agrees to the suggestion of Gradka Bonescu, the Mixo-Lydian Ambassadress, to dine together (*The Duke's Daughter* 192). Thirkell, after writing that "We do not wish to be unkind to Mr. Harvey. No: this is not quite true. We should dearly love to be unkind to him, but if noblesse oblige, so does middle class," then creates a long passage touting how awful Geoffrey is, one of the very few instances in the Barsetshire series in which the author takes more than a few words to excoriate a character (194-95); here, Thirkell's virulent expression of dislike is reminiscent of her remarks about Una Grey in *High Rising*, in both instances inadvertently crossing the line into making the other characters look cruel and creating sympathy for the object of all the dislike. When Gradka follows up with extreme rudeness to some very mild remarks by Geoffrey about the importance of his work in time of war, he does not respond in kind but rather says how delightful the lunch has been and excuses himself to get back to his office (195-97). One might think that a mild answer would turneth away wrath, but in the case of Geoffrey Harvey it does not.

Some years later, Sir Robert Fielding brings the Harveys in to visit the Crawleys after a dinner party. Not only does the Dean make a negative face, but pretty Mrs. Joram, she who was Mrs. Brandon, is deliberately rude to Geoffrey, who is "bowled over by her" (*What Did It Mean?* 250). He is perhaps considerably less charmed when she praises the Mixo-Lydian Ambassadress (who was so very rude to Geoffrey in *The Duke's Daughter*), but in typical Geoffrey Harvey fashion, he responds politely, making a little joke in Latin about people having different tastes, whereupon Mrs. Joram catches him up, presses him as to his remark's literal meaning, and appeals to Dean Crawley as the real expert (*What Did It Mean* 251). Dean Crawley is unsure of the meaning, so Geoffrey tries to ease the moment with another little joke against himself, "Then my wretched ignorance is the less blameable," whereupon the Dean glares at him (251).

Geoffrey's gentle nature finally can be summed up in the fact that in *Marling Hall* he cannot even be firm about the chickens, which he hates: Thirkell has a wonderful description of both Mrs. Marling and Lucy masterfully ordering the Harveys to keep chickens, while Geoffrey desperately and ineffectually tries to block that plan (86-92). As owners of the chickens, both Harveys are sneered at by the author for "having the intellectual's humanitarian feelings towards animals on whom kindness is entirely wasted" (*Marling Hall* 227). In the end, Barsetshire's rejection of Geoffrey Harvey in every way is more overt than is his rejection of Barsetshire, but as he thinks to himself (he is far too polite to say so aloud) at the beginning of *Marling Hall*, "to live among barbarians in the provinces was no part of his plan" (50). He has not changed his mind by the end, when he feels it is "Better far to leave these barbarians to their own society and return to the shades of Whitehall" (299).

Works Cited

Burrell, Barbara. *Angela Thirkell's World: A Guide to the People and Places of Barsetshire*. Wakefield, RI: Moyer-Bell, 2001.

Snowden, Cynthia. *Going to Barsetshire*. Kearny, Nebraska: Morris Publishing, 2000.

Thirkell, Angela. *August Folly*. London: Hamish Hamilton, 1936.

Thirkell, Angela. *County Chronicle*. London: Hamish Hamilton, 1950.

Thirkell, Angela. *The Duke's Daughter*. London: Hamish Hamilton, 1951.

Thirkell, Angela. *High Rising*. London: Hamish Hamilton, 1933.

Thirkell, Angela. *Love Among the Ruins*. Wakefield, Rhode Island: Moyer Bell, 1997 [orig. 1948].

Thirkell, Angela. *Marling Hall*. London: Hamish Hamilton, 1942.

Thirkell, Angela. *Peace Breaks Out*. Wakefield, RI: Moyer Bell, 1997 [orig. 1946].

Thirkell, Angela. *What Did It Mean?* London: Hamish Hamilton, 1954.

Thirkell, Angela. *Wild Strawberries*. London: Hamish Hamilton, 1934.

Contributor

Penelope Fritzer earned her B. A. in History from Connecticut College and her Ph. D. in English from the University of Miami. She is the author of numerous education articles and of six books: *Jane Austen and Eighteenth-Century Courtesy Books*, *Ethnicity and Gender in the Barsetshire Novels of Angela Thirkell*, *Merry Wives and Others: A History of Domestic Humor Writing* (with Bart Bland), *Social Studies Content for Elementary and Middle School Teachers*, *Science Content for Elementary and Middle School Teachers* (with Valerie Bristor), and *Mathematics for Elementary and Middle School Teachers* (with Barbara Ridener). She discovered Angela Thirkell through a column by Dee Hardie and has addressed the Angela Thirkell Society national meetings several times. She is a Professor at Florida Atlantic University, where she teaches English and Social Studies Methods.

**Three Contemporaries:
Comparing Dorothy L. Sayers,
D. E. Stevenson and Georgette
Heyer with Angela Thirkell
by
Jerri Jazbinschek Chase**

In the Autumn of 2003, Angela Thirkell Society North America members received a survey asking for information about favorite authors, books and mysteries. When the survey results were compiled, in the section labeled "Top Selections" were several British contemporaries of Angela Thirkell. Three of them are Dorothy L. Sayers, D. E. Stevenson and Georgette Heyer.

All four authors, including Thirkell, were born near the turn of the nineteenth/twentieth century, early enough to remember and to have been impacted by World War I. Dorothy Emily Stevenson was born in Edinburgh Scotland and the rest in England. Angela Mackail (later, Thirkell) was the eldest, having been born in 1890. D.E. Stevenson was born in 1892 and Dorothy L. Sayers in 1893. Georgette Heyer was the youngest of the four, born in 1902. However, since Heyer's first published work appeared when she was very young, their writing lifetimes all overlapped.

All four women were "first borns." Thirkell had a younger brother and sister, Stevenson a younger sister, and Heyer two brothers. Sayers was an only child, but according to

Barbara Reynolds, when cousins or children of family friends came to spend some time in their household to study with the Sayers' family governesses, Dorothy could and did boss them around and lead the activities as if she were an older sister.

These writers were all born to educated parents and into middle or upper middle class families, not into the top tier of society and not into the bottom. Angela Mackail was the granddaughter of the artist Sir Edward Burne-Jones, and cousin to both author Rudyard Kipling and prime minister Stanley Baldwin.

D.E. Stevenson's family background could be considered closest to the young Angela Mackail's, with its mixture of art, writing and politics. Stevenson's father was a first cousin to Robert Louis Stevenson, and the Stevenson family of engineers was prominent in Scotland, having been responsible for the building of all the lighthouses on the coast of Scotland. Her mother was closely related to Frederick Roberts, Field Marshall Lord Roberts of Kandahar, who had a prominent place in the British military and political system. Stevenson later acquired ties to the artistic world by marrying a "Peploe", whose uncle was Samuel John Peploe, R.S.A., N.P.S., an oil painter and one of the "Scottish Colourists".

Dorothy L. Sayers was the daughter of a Church of England clergyman, who was teaching in a boys' school in Oxford at the time she was born. He then moved the family to East Anglia where he became a rector. Georgette Heyer's father was a Cambridge educated schoolteacher,

Timeline
Angela Thirkell – Dorothy L. Sayers – D. E. Stevenson – Georgette Heyer

1890	1910	1920	1930
|	|	|!	|

Thirkell 1912-s1914-s1917-18-dt 1921-s
1890-birth 1911-m 1917-d1918-m1920-to Australia
1921----------------- 1931-
magazine *Three*
publications *Houses*

Sayers 1924-s 1926-marriage
1893-birth 1916,1918 1923-----------------------
poetry 12
mysteries,30+short
stories,ed.
anthol.Lord Peter

Stevenson 1916-m,dt 1918-s 1922-dt 1928-*dt dies* 1932-s
1892-birth 1915 1923 1926 1932--
poetry 1st novel poetry novel

Heyer 1925-marriage
1932-s
1902-birth 1921---------------------------
book publications,
av.1 per
year, mix historical
fiction

|	|	|	|
1890	1910	1920	1930

m=marriage d=divorce s=birth of son dt=birth of daughter

Timeline

Angela Thirkell – Dorothy L. Sayers – D. E. Stevenson – Georgette Heyer

```
                              1959-w 1960-death
--------------------------------------------1959  +    1961
book publications, average one              Three Score
per year, mostly Barsetshire                and Ten
```

```
                  1950-w 1957-death
1937-------------------------------1957                   1972,73
1998
   plays, translations, etc.                   previously unpublished
Thrones
                                               Lord Peter stories
Dominations
```

```
                                        1969-w   1973-death
-------------------------------------------------------------1970
successful novel publications, average 1 per year
many interrelated characters and settings
```

```
                                                  1974-death
--------------------------------------------------------1972    1975
book publication continues, mix historical fiction          My Lord
John
romance, mysteries, best known for regencies
```

w=widowed

and her mother had been an outstanding student in cello and piano at the Royal College of Music, giving up her career upon her marriage.

All four seem to have received educations typical of females of that time and class. Family was a strong influence, and they also had governesses. All but D.E. Stevenson spent at least some time in either day schools or boarding schools. Their schooling seemed to concentrate on broad reading, literature, humanities, history, classics and languages. All would one day have the characters in their novels quote frequently and casually from a broad spectrum of many of the same authors: Dickens, Jane Austen, Shakespeare, etc. and use French, Latin and other foreign language phrases without feeling the need to translate for the reader. Dorothy L. Sayers was the only one to go to University, being one of the first group of women to receive degrees at Oxford. D.E. Stevenson passed the admissions test for Oxford, but her parents decided not to allow her to attend.

There is some evidence of early efforts at writing by all four. Angela Mackail apparently wrote stories and poems at Rottingdean in her childhood. She also wrote for school publications. The young Dorothy L. Sayers wrote plays in which family and friends acted, as well as poetry, and when she went to boarding school, she wrote more plays and items for school publications. D. E. Stevenson is said to have started writing stories and poems as early as age eight, and Georgette Heyer told stories to amuse her younger brothers, and since a serial story she wrote to entertain her brother Boris while he was ill was published when she was nineteen, she must have started writing them down at an early age.

Photographs of all four authors in their teens and twenties show attractive and striking young women. Margot Strickland says that Angela Thirkell was proud of her long, graceful neck shown in the Sergent charcoal, and Barbara Reynolds notes Sayers was called "Swanny" at boarding school, as her friends teased her about the length of her neck.

All of the subjects married, Thirkell twice: like George Thirkell, James Reid Peploe and Oswold Arthur (Mac) Fleming (the husbands of D. E. Stevenson and D. L. Sayers) were World War I veterans. All four women became mothers: Heyer and Sayers each had one son. Stevenson, like Thirkell, had four children, but only three lived to grow up. For both Thirkell and Stevenson, their youngest child was a son, several years younger than the others, who could be considered his mother's favorite.

Thirkell's first publications did not appear until after her second marriage, and all were published using her married name. The other three authors all had at least some work published prior to marriage, and all three published their works using their maiden names. All but Stevenson also had posthumous publications.

The need for money was certainly at least one motivation for all of them to write for publication, so the reader can consider each author's situation and accomplishments in this light. By the late 1920s, George Thirkell had become unemployed and was no longer a source of support. Thirkell had a young son, completely dependent, and two older sons whom she helped from time to time, and she had written for various publications, starting in 1921, while she was living in Australia with her husband. Some of these early writings were in Australian publications and some in

English ones. After her return to England in 1929, she started writing books. She needed money, first to reduce her dependence on her parents and friends, and eventually to provide complete financial independence. Her first book, the autobiographical *Three Houses*, was followed by novels, a biography and a children's book. Eventually she found her way to writing books set in Barsetshire, and started the "one Barsetshire book per year" pattern she was to follow until her death. She produced twenty-eight Barsetshire books, and the additional Barsetshire book left uncompleted at her death was finished by C. A. Lejeune and published as *Three Score and Ten* in 1961.

Dorothy L. Sayers was the only one of these four authors to have paid employment, other than writing, and she had a variety of jobs after completing her university education. She worked in publishing, taught, and for nine years was in advertising, but these jobs apparently didn't pay well enough to support a single woman, since she received financial assistance from her parents until her Lord Peter novels became successful. She wrote the first several Lord Peter novels while working in her advertising job at Bensons, where her efforts in promotional programs for Guinness and The Mustard Club were well known. Also, at this time she became pregnant, and the father of the child turned out to be both married and unwilling (and probably unable) to provide financial assistance. She was concerned that public knowledge of her pregnancy would result in the loss of her job and in discomfort for her clergyman father. She managed to keep her family, friends and employers in ignorance of her pregnancy, and went away for the birth of her son. She then arranged to pay to have him raised by a cousin, so the financial success of her books became even more important.

While still working at Bensons, but after Lord Peter had made his print appearance, Sayers met "Mac" Fleming, a divorced World War I veteran, whom she married. The early years of their marriage were happy, but he was in and out of work, and as his physical and emotional problems became worse, he became more of a burden than a partner. However, the success of her books allowed Sayers to leave her job to write full time. Her father's death in 1928 left her the head of the family, with the care of her mother and elderly aunt in addition to her husband and son.

By 1936-37 Sayers started transferring her major writing projects from detective fiction to plays, and from plays to religious writings, essays and translations. However, in the fifteen or so years she wrote detective fiction she produced twelve novels (eleven of them about Lord Peter) and over thirty short stories. She also worked on several joint projects with other members of the Detection Club and edited three major collections of detective and horror fiction. An unfinished Lord Peter novel, *Thrones, Dominations* was completed by Jill Paton Walsh and published in 1998. This was followed by *A Presumption of Death*, loosely inspired by "The Wimsey Papers," articles about the family she wrote during the early days of World War II for *The Spectator*

When D. E. Stevenson married James Reid Peploe in 1916, he was a captain in the British Army, on medical leave from service in World War I. They had three children by 1922 and a fourth child in 1930. Stevenson's sister married into the Chambers publishing family, allowing Stevenson's novel, *Peter West*, to be serialized in *The Chambers Journal*, and published by Chambers in book form in 1923, but it was not a success. In the early 1930s, Stevenson started the highly successful Miss Buncle and Mrs. Tim series, and by 1940 she had eleven books in print. It is likely that a major portion of the costs of such things as boarding schools for the three surviving children and the nice house they purchased were supplied by Stevenson's successful writing career. She eventually published a total of forty-five novels, plus some children's poetry.

Georgette Heyer's first book was published in 1921 when she was only nineteen years old. Her father felt that the story, written to amuse her brother during a period of illness, was worthy of publication, and helped her deal with an agent and publisher. She wrote steadily after that, and had published five books by 1925. However, in that year the financial need to write increased, as her father died shortly before her marriage, leaving her to support her mother and her youngest brother, Frank, who was in his mid teens.

Early in their married life, Heyer's husband George Ronald Rougier worked as a mining engineer, traveling to out of the way places like the Caucasus and Macedonia. Sometimes she traveled with him and sometimes she stayed in England. He eventually became a barrister, but for many years Heyer's writing was the major source of income for the family. Over a writing career of some fifty years, Heyer produced four contemporary romance novels, forty historical novels (most with at least an element of romance), twelve thrillers, and a book of short stories, as well as some assorted articles for various magazines.

What if anything is similar about these authors' actual writings? First and foremost, they all wrote character driven novels, and each of them has acquired multigenerational followers who think of the authors' characters as real people, with lives before and after publication. There is reason to believe that even the authors considered their characters to have an "existence" of sorts outside of the published books. Thirkell enjoyed "going to Barsetshire" with selected friends, discussing what characters were doing. Sayers both talked and wrote about the history of Lord Peter's family (see *The Wimsey Family* by C.W. Scott-Giles) and about what was happening to individuals after she had stopped writing the books. Stevenson is quoted as saying that she knew far more about her characters than she ever had time or space to disclose in her books – their likes, dislikes, history, etc. Heyer, in letters to her publishers and agents, makes it clear that her characters often appear to have minds of their own. Geoffrey Cox notes that all four authors give the reader a strong sense of place. Their books contain frequent evocative, descriptive passages, allowing the reader to "see" the places where the characters are living. Some books by Thirkell, Stevenson, and Sayers include maps to help the reader understand the lay of the land. And when Heyer's characters travel across the English countryside, the modern reader with a detailed map of the area can readily follow their paths.

All four authors depict life in England (and/or Scotland) and include such characters as Church of England vicars, talkative and/or eccentric ladies of "a certain age," elderly relatives, nannies, cooks, and so on. Events such as garden parties, fetes, weddings, bring and buy sales, working parties, and meetings are covered, and humor is very much in order.

Similarly, all four authors used their broad educations in the humanities to create characters who quote and refer to great literature of the past. These references have stimulated the publication of companion books, such as

Cynthia Snowden's *Going to Barsetshire* and Stephen P. Clark's *The Lord Peter Wimsey Companion*, both of which provide references to these quotations and explain terms which have become obscure with the passage of time, as well as providing other services to readers. Fans of Heyer and Stevenson, working together aided by the internet, are currently working on projects to collect similar information about the works of these two authors.

All four of these authors used experiences from their own lives as inspiration for their novels. For example, Thirkell used places she had stayed and people she had met to inspire characters and towns in her books, as is described by Margot Strickland in *Angela Thirkell, Portrait of a Lady Novelist*. Sayers used her experiences working in advertising in her novel *Murder Must Advertise*, and she used her vacations with her husband in Scotland for the location for *Five Red Herrings*. D. E. Stevenson's popular *Mrs. Tim* series was based on her personal experiences as wife of a serving military officer, and in later life her personal travel would inspire some of her characters to make similar trips. Heyer's early books are very autobiographical, in much the same way as *Ankle Deep* and *O, These Men These Men* were for Thirkell, and as Heyer lived in or visited various parts of England, the locations used in her historical romances expanded to include the places she had been.

Books by these authors show the reader aspects of English culture and how it was changed by World War II and its aftermath, often using a series with continuing characters. Thirkell, in her Barsetshire books, creates a world in which the reader meets the same people and places over and over at various times. In Barsetshire, which she took from Anthony Trollope, one can get glimpses of life before, during and after World War II, and can see how the changes caused by a combination of the war and advent of "modern times" impacted characters' lives.

Sayers' detective novels all take place prior to World War II, and all but one have Lord Peter (Wimsey) as the hero, with other continuing characters. In *Gaudy Night* and *Thrones, Dominations,* the impending war is seen, and "The Wimsey Papers" offer interesting insight into the early impact of World War II.

While D. E. Stevenson's novels take place in various parts of England and Scotland (with occasional short excursions to foreign parts such as Rome, Egypt, Denmark, etc.), most of them are "connected" in some way, with characters from one book appearing or being mentioned in another. Children in different books may attend the same boarding school, a doctor from one book attends the birth of a baby in another book when the local doctor is unavailable, the minister who speaks in the absence of the local minister or helps with a funeral is often someone the reader knows from a different book, and there are also some direct sequels and series. Changes brought on by the war and its aftermath are shown. Heyer's thrillers and contemporary novels offer some direct insight into England during the pre- and post-World War II periods.

Each author wrote some of her works from a male point of view. Angela Thirkell did this in *Trooper to the Southern Cross* and also to an extent in *Summer Half,* largely the tale of Colin Keith and his friends and mentors, Everard Carter and Noel Merton. Most of Dorothy L. Sayers' *Lord Peter* books are written from Lord Peter's point of view. And both Heyer and Stevenson wrote some of their books wholly or in major part from the point of view of male characters, for Heyer *The Foundling, The Toll-gate,* and *The Unknown Ajax,* and for Stevenson *Green Money, Gerald and Elizabeth,* and *Five Windows.*

Sayers seems to have been the only one of the four who didn't struggle with dust jacket issues. In England her major publisher was Victor Gollancz, whose rather loud yellow jackets with bold red and black lettering didn't allow much individuality. From Sayers's collected letters one can read much discussion of plot development, but none about dust jackets.

Strickland avers that Thirkell was concerned about the appearance of her dust jackets and often worked quite hard to get what she wanted. When she once wrote that she didn't care if they were yellow like Gollancz', she was certainly being ironic. D.E. Stevenson was concerned about her dust jackets as well, becoming irritated, for example, when the blond heroine of one book was pictured with dark hair on the English dust jacket. In the United States, Stevenson had the vast majority of her dust jackets produced by John O'Hara Cosgrave II, and many of Thirkell's American dust jackets were also by Cosgrave. Heyer, too, was very concerned that dust jackets be correct in their image of her books. She demanded correct period detail in the illustrations, and eventually found an artist, Barbosa, who did many dust jacket illustrations for her for various publishers and for books published on both sides of the Atlantic.

A final common ground is what one might call moral attitudes. Diana McFarlan says in *Delicious Prose*:

> Two fellow Scotswomen I find particularly interesting to compare with Angela Thirkell. I compare

them not because the two wrote often about English people in an English county . . . but because they too impose their strong opinions and standards on the reader with hidden force and persuasiveness equal to that of Mrs. Thirkell. The first is the 'mistress of the light novel' Dorothy Emily Peploe who wrote under her maiden name D. E. Stevenson. How deceptive is her simple style and her apparently ordinary stories. In nearly forty novels, not all of equal strength, she tells extremely interesting tales of relatively ordinary people in England or Scotland. In these she puts over with an assurance equal to that of Mrs. Thirkell the excellent standards of the Scottish gentlewoman and persuades one to her own opinions of goodness and badness. Her plots are always as interesting as her characters and they are described with a statement of facts that looks naïve but is really a very subtle form of setting the scene. In this they resemble Mrs. Thirkell's Barsetshire novels, but neither writer influenced each other in the very least, if they ever read each other's works. The resemblance is in the imposition of the writer's standards upon the reader; in the case of D. E. Stevenson particularly it is morality without tears or effort. One can truly say that the pleasure she has given to countless readers equals that supplied over the same years by the Barsetshire novels; and that both ladies had the same supreme confidence in the way they were brought up and in the standards they uphold.

(McFarlan 122-23)

The other Scotswoman referred to was Jane Duncan, author of the "My Friend" series. While both Stevenson and Thirkell were firmly upholding similar standards, there were some differences. For example, Thirkell's characters make their feelings plain on many issues, including the war, the government, the servants, development and "progress." Stevenson's characters often have similar thoughts, but their reticence doesn't usually allow them to express their feelings in such outspoken ways.

Stevenson's characters show more concern for the needs and feelings of others than do Thirkell's. For example, in the end of *Listening Valley*, published in 1944, the heroine worries not only about the fighter pilot to whom she has just become engaged, but also about all the splendid men on both sides who were being killed each day and the wives and mothers who would be heavy-hearted on their behalf. It is hard to imagine one of Thirkell's characters voicing such concerns.

Dorothy L. Sayers directly addressed moral issues in her religious plays and writings. However, a close reading of her detective fiction shows that she also imposed a moral framework on the world she created:

> Moral fiction – that is, fiction that probes the meaning of good and evil – is not limited to writers with a clearly religious slant, of course. A writer can be interested in exploring what constitutes moral action without reference to a supreme arbiter outside of human experience. In the case of Dorothy L. Sayers, however, her fiction is informed by Christian assumptions about sin and salvation, guilt and responsibility, and the implied definition of right conduct that emerges in her created world reflects the Christian dogma she accepted as the essential truth of the universe.   (Kenney 192)

The reader is also expected to accept Lord Peter's assumptions of what is "good taste" as well. The proper shoes should be worn to a cricket match, the proper clothing to a formal dinner. The Thirkell fan might see that Lord Peter's style corresponds to that in the better Barsetshire families, and if he had shown up for a sports day at Southbridge School (or in Stevenson's *Summerhills*), he would have fit in well.

The careful reader of Heyer's period romances will find that they are set in a world with its own moral values and views of what constitutes proper behavior – a blend of those Heyer grew up with in early twentieth-century England and those she found in her researching into history:

> She must have recognized this problem at an early stage and solved it brilliantly by retreating into her private Regency world, which had snobbery built in, historical and therefore respectable. We are all snobs of some kind, and it is comfortable to find oneself in a world where the rules are so clearly established, where privilege and duty go hand in hand, and a terrible mockery awaits anyone who takes advantage of position. This is a world, like that of Shakespeare's comedies, where laughter is the touchstone and the purifier, where exposure to the mockery of one's equals is punishment enough equally for Montagu Revesby in *Friday's Child* or Parolles in *All's Well that Ends Well*.
>
> (Hodge 49)

Similarly, this is so for Sir Ogilvy Hibberd in Thirkell's *Before Lunch*. This, then, may be one major underlying assumption common to all four writers works: a good "proper" gentleman (or gentlewoman) has obligations and these must be carried out by their protagonists. Is it this sense of responsibility readers who love these four authors find lacking in much modern fiction? The works of these four authors are very different in some ways, but share a moral core.

On the attached lists of Stevenson and Heyer books supplied, certain titles are marked "not recommended as first reads." These are the books that are atypical, or, in a few cases, sequels so dependant on the early books in the series that they do not stand well alone. Sayers' non-mystery writings arc outside the scope of this paper, but the Lord Peter novels should be read in order of publication, if possible, simply because his personality and his relationships do develop with time. *Miss Buncle's Book* is a good potential first D. E. Stevenson. It deals with an issue that Thirkell herself faced and it is among the more overtly funny of Stevenson's books, with a satirical view of the world that should appeal. Readers who especially enjoy the war time Thirkell novels might enjoy seeing another view of the same events in the wartime Stevenson novels: *The English Air, Mrs. Tim Carries On, Spring Magic, Celia's House, Listening Valley,* or *The Four Graces.* Georgette Heyer wrote books of many different types. Contemporary romances, serious historical fiction, contemporary mysteries, adventure books patterned after The Scarlet Pimpernel, and regency comedies of manners are some of the major classifications. *An Infamous Army,* in which the battle of Waterloo is a prominent feature, is so accurate that it has been used to teach students at Sandhurst about that battle, while other parts of the book are very much romantic fiction. Her serious historical novels are very well researched, but are perhaps less entertaining to some than her lighter fiction where the characters aren't hindered by fact.

Dorothy L. Sayers Books:

Mystery Novels
Whose Body (1923)
Clouds of Witness (1926)
Unnatural Death (1927) (The Dawson Pedigree)
Unpleasantness at the Bellona Club (1928)
Documents in the Case (1930)
     [With Robert Eustace]– not Lord Peter
Strong Poison (1930)
Five Red Herrings (1931) (Suspicious Characters)
Have His Carcase (1932)
Murder Must Advertise (1933)
The Nine Tailors (1934)
Gaudy Night (1935)
Busman's Honeymoon (1937)
Thrones, Dominations (1998)
     [completed by Jill Paton Walsh]

Mystery Short Story Collections
Lord PeterViews The Body (1928)
Hangman's Holiday (1933)
In the Teeth of the Evidence (1939)
Lord Peter (1972)
Striding Folly (1973)

Detection Club Collaborations
The Floating Admiral (1931)
Ask a Policeman (1933)
Six Against the Yard (1936)
The Anatomy of Murder (1936)
Double Death (1939)
No Flowers by Request (1953)

Edited Mystery Anthologies

Omnibus of Crime (Great Short Stories of Detection,
	Mystery & Horror)(1929)
Second Omnibus of Crime (Great Short Stories of
	Detection, Mystery & Horror 2nd series)(1931)
Third Omnibus of Crime (Great Short Stories of
Detection, Mystery & Horror 3rd Series)(1935)

D. E. Stevenson Books:
*Not recommended as first Stevenson

*Peter West (1923)
Mrs. Tim of the Regiment (1932)
Golden Days (1934)
Miss Buncle's Book (1934)
*Divorced from Reality (1935)
	(Miss Dean's Dilemma, The Young Clementina)
*Smouldering Fire (1935)
Miss Buncle Married (1936)
*The Empty World (1936)
	(The World in Spell)
*The Story of Rosabelle Shaw (1937)
	(Rosabelle Shaw)

*Miss Bun the Baker's Daughter (1938)
	(The Baker's Daughter)
Green Money (1939)
Rochester's Wife (1940)
The English Air (1940)
Mrs. Tim Carries On (1941)
Spring Magic (1941)
*Crooked Adam (1942)
Celia's House (1943)
*The Two Mrs. Abbotts (1943)
Listening Valley (1944)
The Four Graces (1946)

*Kate Hardy (1947)
Mrs. Tim Gets a Job (1947)
Young Mrs. Savage (1948)
Vittoria Cottage (1949)
Music in the Hills (1950)
Winter and Rough Weather (1951)
    (Shoulder the Sky)
Mrs. Tim Flies Home (1952)
Five Windows (1953)
Charlotte Fairlie (1954)

(Blow the Wind Southerly, The Enchanted Isle)
Amberwell (1955)
Summerhills (1956)
The Tall Stranger (1957)
Anna and her Daughters (1958)
Still Glides the Stream (1959)
The Musgraves (1960)
Bel Lamington (1961)
Fletchers End (1962)
The Blue Sapphire (1963)
Katherine Wentworth (1964)
Katherine's Marriage (1965)
    (The Marriage of Katherine)
The House on the Cliff (1966)
Sarah Morris Remembers (1967)
Sarah's Cottage (1968)
Gerald and Elizabeth (1969)
The House of the Deer (1970)

Georgette Heyer Books
    *Contempory romance
    #Contempory mystery
    **Serious historical novel

+Not recommended as first Heyer:

The Black Moth (1921)
+Powder and Patch (1923)
      (The Transformation of Philip Jettan)
+The Great Roxhythe (1923)
* +Instead of the Thorn (1923)
+Simon the Coldheart (1925)
These Old Shades (1926)
* +Helen (1928)
The Masqueraders (1928)
* +Pastel (1929)
+Beuvallet (1929)
* +Barren Corn (1930)
** +The Conqueror (1931)
Devil's Cub (1932)
+Footsteps in the Dark (1932)
#Why Shoot a Butler? (1933)
The Convenient Marriage (1934)
#The Unfinished Clue (1934)
+Regency Buck (1935)
#Death in the Stocks (1935)

(Merely Murder)
The Talisman Ring (1936)
#Behold, Here's Poison (1936)
** +An Infamous Army (1937)
#They Found Him Dead (1937)
** +Royal Escape (1938)
#A Blunt Instrument (1938)
#No Wind of Blame (1939)
** +The Spanish Bride (1940)

The Corinthian (1940)

(Beau Wyndham)
Faro's Daughter (1941)
#Envious Casca (1941)
+Penhallow (1942)
Friday's Child (1944)
The Reluctant Widow (1946)
The Foundling (1948)
Arabella (1949)
@The Grand Sophy (1950)
The Quiet Gentleman (1951)
#Duplicate Death (1951)
@Cotillion (1953)
#Detection Unlimited (1953)
@The Toll-Gate (1954)
Bath Tangle (1955)
Sprig Muslin (1956)
April Lady (1957)
Sylvester: or the Wicked Uncle (1957)
@Venetia (1958)
@The Unknown Ajax (1959)
+Pistols for Two (1960) [short stories]
+A Civil Contract (1961)
@The Nonsuch (1962)
@False Colours (1963)
@Frederica (1965)
Black Sheep (1966)
+Cousin Kate (1968)
Charity Girl (1970)
Lady of Quality (1972)
** +My Lord John (1975)

Carroll, David. "Dear Miss Moffat" *Scottish Field*, pp. 41, 46. January 1992

Clark, Stephen P. compiler and editor. *The Lord Peter Wimsey Companion*, 2nd edition. Hurstpierpoint, West Sussex: The Dorothy L. Sayers Society. 2002.

Collins, Laura Roberts. *English Country Life in the Barsetshire Novels of Angela Thirkell, Contributions to the Study of World Literature, number 57.* Westport Connecticut: Greenwood Press, 1994.

Cox, Geoffrey. "Barsetshire, a Sense of Place" *Journal of the Angela Thirkell Society.* No. 24, 2004.

Fahnestock-Thomas, Mary. *Georgette Heyer: A Critical Retrospective.* Saraland Alabama: PrinnyWorld Press, 2001.

Fritzer, Penelope. *Ethnicity and Gender in the Barsetshire Novels of Angela Thirkell.* Westport, Connecticut: Greenwood Press, 1999.

Hodge, Jane Aiken. *The Private World of Georgette Heyer* London: Bodley Head. 1984.

Hogg, Geraldine. "An Appreciation of D. E. Stevenson" unpublished manuscript.

Kenney, Catherine. *The Remarkable Case of Dorothy Sayers* Kent Ohio: Kent State University Press, 1990.

MacLeod, Helen. "Dorothy L. Sayers with Complete Bibliography" *Book and Magazine Collector* . No. 12, pp. 42-49. February 1985

"The Novels of Angela Thirkell" *Book and Magazine Collector.* No. 32, pp. 24-31. November 1986.

McFarlan, D.M. *Delicious Prose: A Study of the Barsetshire Novels of Angela Thirkell.* (no place of publication or publisher listed) 1986.

Peploe, Robin. "The Novels of D. E. Stevenson" *Book and Magazine Collector* No. 104, pp. 32-39, November 1992.

Reynolds, Barbara. *Dorothy L. Sayers : Her Life and Soul.* New York: St. Martin's Press, 1993.

Reynolds, Barbara. ed. *The Letters of Dorothy L. Sayers: 1899 to 1936: The Making of a Detective Novelist.* New York: St. Martin's Press, 1996.

Reynolds, Barbara. ed. *The Letters of Dorothy L. Sayers, Volume Two: 1937 to 1943: From Novelist to Playwright.* New York: St. Martin's Press, 1998.

Scott-Giles, C. W. *The Wimsey Family: A Fragmentary History* compiled from *correspondence with Dorothy L. Sayers* New York: Harper & Row. 1977.

Snowden, Cynthia. *Going to Barsetshire: A Companion to the Barsetshire Novels of Angela Thirkell.* Kearney, Nebraska: Morris Publishing, 2000.

Stevenson, D. E., unpublished manuscripts from collection at Boston University.

Stevenson, D. E., unpublished manuscripts from files of D.E. Stevenson's family.

Strickland, Margot. *Angela Thirkell: Portrait of a Lady Novelist.* Kearney Nebraska: Angela Thirkell Society North American Branch, 1977.

Swallow, Rosemary (daughter of D.E. Stevenson) and family, personal communications, August/ September 2003.

Thirkell, Angela. *Three Houses.* Wakefield Rhode Island: Moyer Bell, 1998. [orig. 1931]

Thirkell, Lance. *Melbourne and London: A Childhood Memoir.* London: Angela Thirkell Society, 2000.

Web Sites:

Angela Thirkell Society: http://www.angelathirkellsociety.com
Angela Thirkell Society North American Branch:
http://www.angelathirkell.org
D.E. Stevenson: http://DEStevenson.org/
http://www.anglophilebooks.com/stevenso.htm
http://www.geocities.com/Heartland/Garden/1024
Dorothy L. Sayers Society: http://www.sayers.org.uk/
Georgette Heyer: http://www.georgette-heyer.com/

Contributor

Jerri Chase earned B. S. degrees in Chemistry and Mathematics from School of the Ozarks and earned an M. S. degree in Library and Information Science from the University of Illinois. She has been a member of the Angela Thirkell Society for many years, addressing the Society at several national meetings. She lives in rural Arkansas and has visited the British Isles several times to see the places associated with the works of English and Scottish authors of the first half of the twentieth century, on which she has done extensive research. She discovered Angela Thirkell through *A Common Reader* catalogue.

Which One Winked, Mrs. Carvel
Or Aubrey Clover?
by
Barbara Houlton

Darling little Jessica Dean tumbled off a donkey when still a baby, and onto the stage when she was grown up. Almost nothing is known about her in the intervening years. Rescued by Richard Tebben from the dangerous bull when she fell in *August Folly*, she indirectly secured a happy future for this miserable young man, and continued to interfere with affairs in Barsetshire for as long as readers maintained their acquaintance with her.   After her introduction in *August Folly,* the only mention of her in the next several books comes in *Growing Up*, when her father runs into Sir Harry Waring (who calls him "Dean"), and concluding the reporting in detail on all the others of his nine children, relates that Jessica is "collecting scrap in her holidays and learning ju-jitsu" (129).

The grown-up Jessica has one characteristic not shared by other females of her Barsetshire generation: a successful career elsewhere. The only other young women who move away do so to be with their husbands, but Jessica emerges as a successful and talented actress in London, with no real indication of how she got there. What motivated Angela Thirkell to take Jessica Dean in this unexpected direction?

Jessica surprises the reader as much as would a magic trick, when she appears in Barsetshire in *Private Enterprise*—not only grown-up and out of school, but having graduated from the Royal Academy of Dramatic Art, toured Australia, traveled to entertain the troops in India during and/or just after the war, and starred at the Cockspur Theatre, without so much of a hint of her activities in Barsetshire. Known in theatrical circles for her famous wink as Mrs. Carvel, she is presented as both talented and charming, always more important characteristics to Angela Thirkell than beauty. Although she spends quantities of time in London with Colin Keith and Oliver Marling, two of Barsetshire's young men about town, they never seem to think to mention her accomplishments to their respective mothers.

As Cynthia Snowden writes in *Going to Barsetshire*, "Any half-awake reader will discern a bit of inconsistency, of age-creep, or perhaps a failure of age to creep in certain characters. How old was Jessica Dean when she burst on the scene as a glamour actress in *Private Enterprise*? ... I'll tell you what (to quote Lucy Marling) it's not very important; don't get out the calculator. The dates are here for fun" (ix-x). Nevertheless, Jessica seems to be somewhere in her early twenties at her reappearance. Although most Thirkell characters hold together logically, the reader may be puzzled by Jessica. How does she run back and forth so easily from London to home, while poor Sir Robert (Graham) can never manage to get home at all? This characteristic of mobility is one which helps to differentiate Jessica from her staid Barsetshire contemporaries.

Without any explicit, prior acquaintance with Lydia Merton, what prompts Jessica in *Private Enterprise* to champion the wifely cause and chide Noel into being the

163

perfect husband? As Noel must be almost twice her age, one can easily imagine him telling her to stay out of his affairs. Nevertheless, she pulls it off, and charms everyone, with a hint of the spoiled brat in her stage performance. As Penelope Fritzer writes, "Jessica is also wise beyond her years, such that she is able to act as a *deux ex machine* for the other characters, swooping down on Barsetshire and setting things right: she reprimands Noel Merton for his treatment of his wife, stops Peggy Arbuthnot from being such a flirt..." (80). Jessica takes advantage of her actress persona to be a personage in her own right in Barsetshire: she is no longer the chubby baby sister.

The Barsetshire Red Cross Fete serves to introduce Jessica's stage partner, Aubrey Clover. Although mentioned in *Private Enterprise* as probably homosexual (Miss Hampton says, "He and I have much in common, only we're on different sides of the fence" with some follow up comments), this characteristic completely disappears in the following books (337). Possibly Thirkell was contemplating a match for Jessica from the available men in Barsetshire, but later dropped the idea.

Whatever his proclivities, Aubrey is immediately acceptable in Barsetshire. Something of a war hero, he is described by Mr. Wickham as rescuing troops from the water at Dunkirk, saving his crew when his little boat is bombed, getting "a bit of shrapnel in his tummy," and subsequently "entertaining the troops all over the place" (*Private Enterprise* 107), while Colin Keith discovers that he and Aubrey served in the war only fifty miles apart (156). Aubrey is presented here as patriotic to the core, and later has a "hideous siren on his car to show Americans what we had to suffer in the war" (209).

In *Love Among the Ruins*, Aubrey and Jessica are visiting the Deans while Aubrey works on his next play. The primary romance is that between Susan Dean and Freddy Belton, centering on the resolution of the romantic mix-up caused by his previous engagement to a W.R.E.N. killed during the war. The plot places Jessica at home, as she and Aubrey are between engagements. It is Aubrey who writes the plays, stars in them, and determines the details of their production, while Jessica is the charming idiot soubrette.

Jessica in *Love Among the Ruins* is very young and playful—she paints ladders on her artificial stockings, and chokes from laughing so hard with Charles Belton, with whom she gets along famously. She behaves as though she is already Barsetshire-engaged to Oliver Marling, as she puts her head on his shoulder, lets her hair fall across his face, and sits at his feet. This amount of physical contact is presumably suitable because she is an actress, but is much closer than that of most of Barsetshire's other engaged couples. Nevertheless, she turns down Oliver's proposal so sweetly that he is in no way dissuaded, but a voice comes out of the dark—"Love's Labours Lost" (451). Both Shakespeare and Aubrey Clover have the last word as the book ends.

This positioning of Jessica and Oliver is particularly interesting because at one point when he proposes, she replies, "There is only one person I could marry. . . . Aubrey. Because he is the Theatre" (*Love Among the Ruins* 402). Her rejection of Oliver, then, is an indicator of Thirkell's intentions for Jessica, who is married to Aubrey before very long. Readers must assume that Thirkell used Jessica and Aubrey as sophisticated counterpoints to the very innocent Barsetshire characters, a technique to help keep her work from becoming dated.

The theatrical association does provide a real connection to post-war London, and a welcome side-plot in the later books. The saga of Jessica and Aubrey continues in more depth in *The Old Bank House*, when Jessica and Aubrey are married, but the marriage is only revealed when the couple arrive for Mr. Adams' house warming at the Old Bank House. Jessica has apparently told her family, since Susan makes casual reference to Jessica's marriage and reveals that their mother is pleased because she likes Aubrey (229). Jessica tells Oliver Marling her news in the gorgeous drawing room while her mother sleeps, whereupon he takes Jessica in his arms (222). This behavior is certainly out of character for Barsetshire, but they are soon parted, and Oliver is talking with Mr. Dean. This is the only book in which Mr. Dean shows a real interest in his children, as he confides to Oliver that he wishes that Jessica had married someone they know better (234-35).

Mr. Dean's mixed emotion on the marriage of his daughter is a repeated theme by Angela Thirkell. All marriages of children in Barsetshire result in parental happiness for their welfare, but also in the knowledge that the era of childhood is over. "We have lost Bob," Dr. Perry says on Bob's marriage in *Happy Returns* (164). Jessica's wedding, like most things that happen to her, is off-stage in *The Old Bank House*, presented after the fact. Aubrey Clover is portrayed in a very positive fashion, and Oliver Marling shakes his hand, liking Aubrey in spite of Oliver's own distress, as Aubrey works very hard at his new role of devoted husband, the only role in which he seems the slightest bit nervous.

Jessica and Aubrey have their first child in *County Chronicle*, Sarah Siddons Clover, born in 1949 (Pate 15).

In the beginning of the book, she is languishing "in an interesting condition" on a sofa at Lucy Marling's wedding reception (88). By the end of the book, Oliver Marling reports that they are taking the baby to America, now in the company of a nurse and Jessica's secretary or maid, Miss M. who is finally given a name in *What Did It Mean?*, Miss Mowbray.

At the end of *County Chronicle*, once again, there are amateur theatricals, as Lady Cora inveigles Aubrey Clover to permit her to perform *Out Goes She*. It is Aubrey Clover on stage in this scene, and not Jessica, as his character is more firmly set. He manages the free performance very firmly with his agent, who wants to collect a fee. This generosity gives readers additional insight into Aubrey's character, as Thirkell wants readers to see him with a personality of his own, as well as in his usual actor's role as befitting to the social scene in Barsetshire. Aubrey is very firmly in control of theatrical, business, and family matters.

In *The Duke's Daughter* Oliver Marling finally gives up his mooning over Jessica after the birth of Sarah Siddons and marries Maria Lufton, who manages him much as she manages her Cocker Spaniels. Thereafter, Thirkell all but drops Jessica and Aubrey from most meaningful plot developments in future books, until *What Did It Mean?* Once again, in *The Duke's Daughter*, Jessica is surprisingly friendly with all the women in Barsetshire, as she has already heard of Oliver's engagement to Maria from Maria herself, when he calls to give her the news. Jessica appears very late in the book, and this time, it is by telephone only. She is gradually disappearing from the Barsetshire scene.

The second child of Aubrey and Jessica, a boy named Henry, is mentioned some years later in *What Did It*

Mean?, but no details are provided. Aubrey Clover gives another of his plays for Barsetshire, this time in honor of the Coronation. As the books progress from *Private Enterprise* to *What Did It Mean?*, Aubrey takes on the stronger role, and Jessica fades more into the background. The innocuous young man from *Private Enterprise* has been replaced by the successful playwright, director and producer. His conversation with Lord Pomfret is long, while Jessica occupies the wings, and the outcome of this party is that young Lord Mellings is written into the Coronation Play. The Clovers spend more time in Barsetshire in *What Did It Mean?* than in any other book, and Aubrey has very much come into his own.

Of course, Jessica still manages to enchant in *What Did It Mean?* This time, her admirer is Ludovic, the teen-age son of Lord and Lady Pomfret. As the Pyramid advertisement proclaims, "Ludovic, the Pomfrets' shy, awkward, talented son, helplessly in love with Jessica Dean...." But the play's the thing, not Jessica, and Ludovic takes a step toward growing up. By 1959 Ludovic looks back at the performance, and, in *Love at All Ages* "his gratitude to Aubrey Clover had overflowed into gratitude to the Mertons..." (62). At this point, and Jessica and Aubrey are referred to as "the Aubrey Clovers" when the young people reminisce: Jessica has disappeared as a separate entity.

Jessica and Aubrey appear finally in *Three Score and Ten*. Incredibly, Mrs. Morland, Lady Bond, and Daphne Bond go to London to see Jessica and Aubrey in a play at the Cockspur Theatre. This is the first time since the denouement of *High Rising* that a trip to London has played a major role in a Thirkell plot. Mrs. Morland greatly enjoys the theatre, but the episode when everyone is there for her birthday party was written not by Thirkell, but by C.

A. Lejeune. In this last of the series, Jessica rarely appears alone without Aubrey, except for a few scattered moments when he is in another room and she is with Oliver Marling. This togetherness is another unique characteristic of this atypical Barsetshire/London couple. Over the years, Aubrey has taken the lead, and Jessica has faded into the background, with only her famous Mrs. Carvel's wink to remind us of her earlier powers.

Readers have always assumed that Angela Thirkell based some of her characters on Anthony Trollope's, and some of her characterizations on real people. Possible models for Aubrey and Jessica have been identified: Noel Coward and Gertrude Lawrence. There is a record of Thirkell seeing a Noel Coward play, *Sigh No More* (Strickland 144), and certainly he fit the model of a multi-talented theatrical personality. Another possibility is Ivor Novello, whose music she loved.

Thirkell has a much closer connection with Novello, who named one of his characters "Madame Koska, a dressmaker," and who admitted to being a fan of Thirkell's, than she does with Coward. The description of Thirkell's and Novello's meeting occurs, however, long after Jessica and Aubrey were invented, although he was certainly a possible candidate for an early model. Novello, born in 1893 and died 1951, had many of the characteristics of Aubrey Clover, although he is less well-known to Americans than is Noel Coward. Novello's obituary avers,

> He was essentially just one of the crowd, from which even his extraordinary gifts could not altogether set him apart. Despite appearances he was at heart always no more nor less than the average member of the audience, and therein lay his strength as a servant

of the public. By making sure of pleasing himself he could safely count on delighting his neighbor. There was nothing here either of condescension or of contrivance. He had but to rely on an instinct that long experience had made almost unerring, and dispense with reason, even good reasons, altogether...

(Novello web site)

This description could also have been written of Aubrey Clover. The model for Jessica Dean is similarly uncertain, and she seems less like Gertrude Lawrence than like Jessie Matthews, who took over the lead from Gertrude Lawrence in 1924 in *Charlot's Review of 1924*. And as Jessica Clover was born Jessica Dean, Jessie Matthews played the role of Susie Dean in the film of Priestley's *The Good Companions*. These two, less well known in the United States, would have been very familiar to Angela Thirkell. Probably, like many of her characters, Jessica Dean and Aubrey Clover were composites of known personalities and of Thirkell's imagination.

Angela Thirkell's interest in the theater was extensive. She loved going to plays, but her books make clear that movies are for the very young and for the lower classes. She wrote only one play, *The Good Little Girls*, a children's play, which was produced in London by a friend. The evidence is that she did not see the production.

Penelope Fritzer provides her analysis of Angela Thirkell's portrayal of the theater: "Much as in Thirkell's own life (and in her presentations of creative people through her books), fame, fortune, and artistic accomplishment are admired but also taken somewhat for granted" (79). Readers and critics have no way of knowing how much or how little Thirkell identified with the theatrical characters—Jessica Dean, Aubrey Clover, and Denis Stoner. She would have a more natural affinity for their world than for the world of country life. Apparently, she attended and loved the theater, with reports from Australia and before of her enchantment, but there are absolutely no reports of her attendance at a pig fair or an agricultural event. When she introduces Jessica Dean in the books, it is her way of indicating that she knows there is a larger world beyond Barsetshire. Perhaps Jessica Dean is a creation of a theatrical daughter for herself, since Jessica Dean's real mother was, of course, -- Angela Thirkell. Angela Thirkell's talented offspring, Jessica, is transformed from the ingénue to the wife and mother valued in Barsetshire, as the stage mother, Angela Thirkell, wraps up her cast of characters for the next generation.

Works Cited

Fritzer, Penelope. *Ethnicity and Gender in the Barsetshire Novels of Angela Thirkell*. Westport, CT: Greenwood Press, 1999.

Glover, William. Private e-mail correspondence, 2004.

Pate, Johnny. *Dictionary of Angela Thirkell's Barsetshire Novels*. Kearney, NE: Angela Thirkell Society, 2000.

Matthews, Jessie.
http://www.btinternet.com/~judyin.london/overmyshoulder/jmhome.htm

Novello, Ivan.http://members.aol.com/Novello/eulogy.html

Snowden, Cynthia. *Going to Barsetshire*. Kearney, NE: Cynthia Snowden, 2000.

Thirkell, Angela. *August Folly*. New York: Carroll & Graf, 1988 [orig. 1936].

Thirkell, Angela. *County Chronicle*.Wakefield, RI: Moyer Bell, 1998 [orig. 1950].

Thirkell, Angela. *Growing Up*. London: Hamish Hamilton, 1943.

Thirkell, Angela. *Happy Returns,* Pyramid Books, Moonachie, N. J. 1973 [orig. 1952].

Thirkell, Angela. *Love at All Ages*. Wakefield, RI: Moyer Bell, 2001 [orig. 1959].

Thirkell, Angela. *Love Among the Ruins*. Wakefield, RI: Moyer Bell, 1997 [orig. 1947].

Thirkell, Angela. *The Old Bank House*. London: Hamish Hamilton, 1949.

Thirkell, Angela. *Private Enterprise*. New York: London, Hamish Hamilton, 1947.

Thirkell, Angela. *What Did It Mean?* New York: Pyramid, 1973 [orig. 1954].

Contributor

Barbara Houlton is the Secretary of the Angela Thirkell Society North America. She has a B. S. degree in Mathematics from Duke University. She lives in San Diego where she works as a private consultant for computer systems. She first became interested in Angela Thirkell after reading Hermione Lee's article in the *New Yorker*, and attended a National meeting, where she and Susan Krzywicki volunteered to construct a web site for the Angela Thirkell Society, www.angelathirkell.org. She became Secretary following Edith Jeude, and in addition to activities associated with the Society, she has most recently been involved with the production of this book.

Women at War
by
Helen Clare Taylor

Readers and critics often think of Angela Thirkell as a chronicler of a way of life gone by. Her rural communities, those small towns and villages which comprise "Barsetshire," and her "county" families--Marlings, Beltons Leslies, Brandons--all become increasingly aware, as the novels progress, that they are representatives of an old order. This change is particularly marked in the novels published after the end of the war in 1945, as the new Labour government elected as a change from Churchill's Conservatives becomes the focus of Thirkell's antagonism to "Them," who stand for vulgarity, mediocrity, cheapness, and lack of caste, everything that the principal families who populate the county oppose. The rise of Sam Adams as Labour Member of Parliament, and his eventual integration into county life through his marriage with Lucy Marling, marks the ascendance of "Them" over the imputed "Us," and reveals Thirkell's sadness over the lost ways of her youth.

It is World War II which heralds this shift for Angela Thirkell. Her seven wartime novels depict a society attempting to pretend that everything is normal, that nothing has changed, and that the usual county standards can survive austerity measures and utility clothing. The stresses of war test Barsetshire's resources, and its routines are disrupted before war has even been declared in September 1939. The preparations for Rose Birkett's wedding in *Cheerfulness Breaks In* reveal how everyone has in mind the repercussions of a "scrap" on the young men of the county. The worsening European political situation results in the Air Raid Precautions Bill (1937) whose aim was to help protect civilians from the effects of aerial bombardment, and which led to the awful Double Summer Time (which causes dinner parties at inappropriate times); to the associated black-out, which is done (often badly) by the various maids; and to the necessity of keeping chickens to supplement the rations, an effort which nearly drives Geoffrey Harvey out of the Red House in *Marling Hall*.

Most usually, however, it is the women who bear the brunt of these strains because they are traditionally in charge of their homes. Thirkell explores the effect of war on the young, such as Lucy Marling and Lydia Keith Merton, and on the old, such as Miss Bunting, the governess. She introduces comic refugees, whose contempt for Barsetshire ways both reinforces the value of those ways to the indignant locals and at the same time gently makes them reassess their positions. The redoubtable Madame Brownscu, for example, highlights the almost forgotten meaning of Christmas when she brings a creche to the children's Christmas party in *Cheerfulness Breaks In* (228). Thirkell also explores the effect of war on the lives of her ordinary upper-middle-class women, as Mrs. Belton, Mrs. Morland, Mrs. Birkett, and Mrs. Brandon, for example, struggle to accommodate the changes brought by their children being in the services, by their homes being used for government purposes, or by the various evacuees being settled in Barsetshire.

The ways Thirkell's women withstand the war, and the ways it threatens to distort their perhaps complacent ideas

174

about home and identity in the county, are particularly important. Thirkell's novels, like many others written at the same time, show how county society provides a home front which responds both willingly and unwillingly to government's policies, and which survives Hitler only to succumb to the evil of "Them."

Thirkell's work falls into a tradition of novels by women about the complex interrelations of families within provincial or rural communities, a tradition that includes Jane Austen and George Eliot. Novels about villages and rural communities were popular during the 1930s: the decade produced many still-widely- read works like *Cold Comfort Farm*, *South Riding*, and the *Provincial Lady* novels. In the context of the war, the village setting becomes a patriotic celebration of the English way of life; Fay Inchfawn in her wartime book *Salute to the Village*, for example, echoes government propaganda in locating the very heart of resistance to the enemy in the resolution of the villagers and in the beauty of the surrounding countryside.

One does not usually think of Angela Thirkell, Barbara Pym, or E. M. Delafield as war novelists, although their work describes what was actually going on in Britain far more acutely than did many of the films made with government assistance which purported to document real life. Against the vast and exciting backdrop of Europe in deadly conflict, these village novels might seem trivial, like Becky Sharpe's flirtation with George Osborne on the eve of the Battle of Waterloo in *Vanity Fair*, but in fact they document significant social history. The enormity of the political situation must have caused Thirkell, who was writing in real time, great unsettledness, as is particularly shown in the last lines of *Cheerfulness Breaks In*, when she holds Noel Merton's fate at Dunkirk in abeyance. Thirkell might well have wondered, like Delafield's narrator in *A Provincial Lady in London,* if as a writer she could contribute to the war effort more immediately than by writing books and "standing by." At the beginning of *Growing Up*, Lady Waring, who is suffering from the general strain and tension of the war, reflects that anxiety in her thoughts:

> . . . how very difficult it must be for people to write novels, because all the young heroines were in the Forces or civilian jobs and all the young heroes the same, so there was very little time for novelists to make them fall in love with each other, unless they made the hero be a flying officer and the heroine a W.A.A.F, and then one would have to know all the details of the R.A.F. or one would make the most dreadful howlers. Unable to find any real solution to this problem, she determined to wait until she saw Mrs. Morland, who wrote a novel every year to earn her living and would be able to tell her exactly how these things were done. (36)

The answer for the novelist is to keep writing the same kinds of books as she has always done: they become a defense against change. Delafield's Provincial Lady is told she can best serve the war effort by keeping public morale high and continuing her fiction. But Thirkell's county stories are not just a way of carrying on as usual; rather, they also provide serious commentary on the domestic effects of war.

British domestic fiction, or fiction about village communities, often engages the crucial philosophical issues pertaining to ordinary life, especially that of women.

Thirkell and the other novelists of her ilk give readers insight into what life at home was really like for women during the war, with its privations as well as its joys. In their works, the villages' struggles to accommodate the necessary disruptions to their routines are less examples of "little England" as valiant underdog, than they are opportunities for women left at home to examine their own roles in the nation's upheaval. The novels' female characters often use the facts of war, with its rationing, evacuations, and loss of male partners, to interrogate their status as full human beings. Lucy Marling, Delia Brandon, Octavia Crawley, and Elsa Belton, for example, are all affected by the need for women to work in civilian and service jobs on an equal footing with men, and their attempts to reconcile their new status with their roles as young county ladies often presents an opportunity for observation of change in women's social roles. At the Deanery dinner party towards the end of *Cheerfulness Breaks In*, Mrs. Crawley looks down the dinner table at her guests and muses to herself on the fate of these young girls in war time:

> Delia and Octavia were diligent at the hospital and never tried to change their hours for the sake of a treat. . the Archdeacon's daughter was training land girls with efficient zeal. . . Lydia Keith. . .was managing the estate and both her parents, beside her other activities. . Would these girls care to marry? How many would lose a lover, a friend that might have been a lover? . . . Were Octavia, Delia, Lydia to go on being nice useful girls forever?   (*Cheerfulness Breaks In* 301-302)

For Mrs. Crawley, one of Thirkell's guardians of the old ways, the young girls are at risk of having their proper social function turned upside down by the war; it is not enough for her that they be "nice, useful girls," even though the war has given them a reason for independence. She does not disapprove of their war work, but she feels that it will have an unalterable effect on women's place in Barsetshire society, and it is this that she regrets.

Given that young women must serve on the home front, however, and despite Mrs. Crawley's misgivings, Thirkell celebrates her young women as hardworking heroines. She emphasizes the prosaic nature of the jobs they do, undertaken with no thought for personal glory but to serve the community and the nation. In contrast, the media then and now would often have people believe that during the war women were only engaged in the glamorous and the unusual. The conscription of men and the need for the economy to be largely supported by women's work characterized the decade from the Munich crisis in 1938 as a period of enhanced public female status. One can read in historical and social criticism about the "larger" themes of women's industrial work, epitomized for the public in films and posters glorifying "Rosie the Riveter," portrayed as a strong, capable woman with muscles in her arm, who is the motor behind the machine of war. Equally celebrated are the hardy Land Girls, who did the work of the British farmers and foresters who had been conscripted. Lydia Merton wants to be a Land Girl at the beginning of *Growing Up*, but is prevented first by one of those abhorrent government rules and then by her responsibilities to her failing parents. These wartime roles for women served the propaganda machine well because they ennobled the idea of "keeping the home fires burning." As Angus Calder points out, the "myth of the Blitz," which has exaggerated and romanticized the British people's nonchalance during raids, has dominated the popular view of what happened on the home front. Thirkell reminds readers, in contrast, that the real heroines were those who did the unremarkable, invisible work, and her novels highlight their achievements in just doing their jobs, whatever those jobs may be.

Whatever gains women had made in the public sphere by becoming essential to the wartime economy through their contributions to the workforce, they were due to lose those gains at the end of the war. The government could not afford to let women keep their jobs when the demobilized soldiers needed to be employed. Moreover, it was important to show that Hitler had not changed England, and that meant keeping women in the home (ironically, one of Hitler's aims too). Robert Mackay comments that the disruptions of 1939-45 "served as much to reinforce as to challenge [women's] traditional roles, leaving at its end a dominant feeling that little had changed, after all" (226). In fact, the austerity of the post-war years, together with the baby boom, created a society in which women were very much at home again, looking after children and managing their houses with little domestic help. Thirkell represents this inward focus as the right course, in opposition to the new order espoused by "Them." Interestingly, in *Growing Up*, Lady Waring becomes uncomfortable at a discussion between Leslie Waring and Lydia Merton about the role of women after the war, in which Leslie espouses the traditionalist view while commenting on her job in a civilian role in London:

I think it is frightening. . . Most of the women I had under me were incredibly efficient and I don't think they were any more trying than the men. But it's all upside down. It is quite horrid not being able to feel that men are superior beings. I'd much rather I did.
(101)

Before any resolution is gained in the discussion, Thirkell has Noel Merton change the subject, for he sees Lady Waring's discomfiture. The reader gets the sense that Thirkell herself is troubled by the argument, and that Lady Waring's concern, like Mrs. Crawley's in the earlier novel, reveals an admiration for women's war time work, and at the same time a regret for the social upheaval it must cause.

The novels allow readers to make up their own minds on this issue by reviewing varied experiences for women during the war. Those who visit Barsetshire from the city are usually either insufferable or spoiled. Like Leslie Waring, Elsa Belton in *The Headmistress* has an important job in town which gives her prestige and cachet. It does not stop her, however, from acting like a child in front of her masterful fiancé, Christopher Hornby. The predatory Frances Harvey who comes with her brother Geoffrey to live at the Red House in *Marling Hall* is drawn by Thirkell as an unattractive bureaucrat, whose London ways and wartime status win her no champions at Marling. And while Mrs. Major Spender has no apparent career except that of embarrassing her long-suffering husband Bobbums, she fatigues the stoic Verena Villars in *Northbridge Rectory* with tedious and cloying detail about how Mrs. Spender has prevailed during the Blitz in London. Opportunities for valor present themselves to these characters, but they are not seized.

Thirkell's two most important war "heroines" have little real role in the home front activities at all, yet they play a crucial part in Thirkell's portrayals of women's war efforts. Lydia Keith would love to take an active part in the war: like her friends Delia Brandon and Octavia Crawley, she wants to nurse hideously wounded soldiers at the hospital.

Yet she sacrifices a more exciting war job to do a job that must be done–taking care of her mother and father, tending the family home, and feeding the abominable evacuees rabbit stews at the communal kitchen. Described throughout *Summer Half* as a "swashbuckling" type, Lydia seems cut out for wartime glamour, but she must shoulder her responsibilities rather than fulfill her dreams. It is this quiet domestic heroism that makes Noel Merton admire and love her in *Cheerfulness Breaks In*, and that is the basis of Thirkell's presentation of Lydia as the best of Barsetshire during war.

Similarly Miss Bunting, the elderly governess who has had so many Barsetshire youth in her charge, is another symbol of the county heritage and its courage in facing not just Hitler but "Them." Lady Fielding remarks to her husband that "Bunny's" death marks the end of Barsetshire as they know it: "[O]ne of the remaining links with the old world of an ordered society had snapped. Nearly everything for which Miss Bunting stood was disintegrating in the great upheaval of civilization" (*Miss Bunting* 310). Miss Bunting's function is exemplified in her recurring wartime dream. Where she dreams that she grows wings and flies to Germany to confront Hitler, whom she asks to spare her old pupils in return for her own life. She knows that if she can keep asleep long enough she can have her way. Each time Miss Bunting wakes too soon, except the last, when she exchanges her life for those of her beloved pupils:

> Alighting in Hitler's dining room just as he was beginning his lunch, she stood in front of him and said "Kill me, but don't kill my pupils, because I can't bear it," adding the words "and if you touch David Leslie, my favorite pupil, I shall kill you." With an immense effort she remained asleep just long enough to be sure

that she had won. Then Hitler swelled and swelled till the whole room and the whole world was full of him and burst, and all Miss Bunting's old pupils came running up to her. Her heart was so full of joy that it stopped beating. (*Miss Bunting* 309)

Miss Bunting's dream and death symbolize her protection of Barsetshire, personified in its hopeful young people whom she has schooled in decorum and manners. In the dream, she must die to ensure victory against Hitler, and so she does, signaling the peace which comes at the expense of the triumph of "Them," rulers of a world in which Miss Bunting and her standards no longer have any place. Thirkell's deft use of symbolism is masterful here as she makes the governess a martyr of the war, saving her pupils but unable to guarantee them a society like that which she upholds.

Barsetshire in war is governed by wise women, but their mettle is surely tested by the organized influx of the groups of strangers which the war brought to small communities. These strangers can be described in three categories. The first, usually attracting comic attention in fiction despite their tragic situation, are the foreign refugees, who had been fleeing Europe for most of the 1930s. These appear in Angela Thirkell's novels as a composite group, the "Mixo-Lydians," whose comic-sounding language and exotic folktales amaze the staid villagers. In *Cheerfulness Breaks In*, readers meet Madame Brownscu and her husband or paramour Gogo (it is never quite clear what his status is) whose only dialogue throughout the book is "Czy, provka, provka, provka," which Madame Brownscu dramatically translates as "No, never, never, never." Each time this couple appears, these words are used in different, improbable situations. Another important Mixo-Lydian is

Gradka Bonescu, the future ambassador, who in *Miss Bunting* acts as the Fieldings' cook and tells the hilarious and awful story of her country's national hero Gradko. Often descriptions of the means by which the foreign women run their new homes provide points of comparison for female characters, and Thirkell's women must hold their own against these foreigners, who in *Cheerfulness Breaks In* try to sell embroidery at exorbitant prices and who do not try to hide their scorn and contempt for Barsetshire.

The second influx of newcomers is made up of the civil servants and military officials whose offices have been moved away from the cities to ensure the continued running of the government. These officials were often billeted on stately or large homes requisitioned for the purpose, like Northbridge Rectory, turning the lady of the house into a landlady. In *Northbridge Rectory*, Verena Villars has to suffer not only Mrs. Major Spender but Captain Hooper as well, and her gentle politeness is often pushed to the limit. The male additions to village society, together with the soldiers from military installations often based nearby, also provide romantic opportunities for the local young women like Mrs. Turner's nieces or like Leslie Waring, much as the soldiers at Meryton attracted the Bennet girls in Jane Austen's *Pride and Prejudice*.

The third important group described in women's wartime fiction is made up of evacuees. The declaration of war in 1939 fractured normal family life for thousands of people; the anticipated blanket-bombing by the Germans mandated the black-out, underground "A.R.P." stations, and, most significantly, the mass evacuation of children from urban to rural areas, all of which combined to enforce new domestic situations. Some whole schools were evacuated together;

in *Cheerfulness Breaks In*, Thirkell describes the Hosiers' Boys' Foundation School, which must share space with Southbridge School, and in *The Headmistress*, she does the same for the Hosiers' Girls' Foundation School, which takes over the Beltons' house under the admirable guidance of Miss Sparling. Other schools include both the comically named St. Bathos and St. Quantock, and the Hiram Road School, whose pupils inspire fear and loathing at the Southbridge Christmas Treat in *Cheerfulness Breaks In*.

For Thirkell, the problematic areas of the evacuations, apart from issues of scheduling and physical location, are issues of class. As twenty-first century Western culture no longer recognizes rigid class distinctions in quite the same way, the modern reader may find some of Thirkell's connection of class with morality distasteful, although Thirkell is generous about individuals. Throughout *Cheerfulness Breaks In*, for example, Mrs. Bissell, the wife of the Hosiers' Boys' Foundation School's principal, has deplorable taste and uses lower middle class language laden with pop psychology, but Thirkell indicates Mrs. Bissell's goodness through that lady's treatment of her pathetic niece Edna, and in her fearless and open-minded discussions with Misses Bent and Hampton on the subject of "vice." While Thirkell's treatment shows Mrs. Bissell's adaptation and quiet heroism, Thirkell does not treat the evacuated male teachers so kindly, especially Mr. Hopkins the science master, who goads Everard Carter to say he never quite knew what "common room" meant before *(Cheerfulness Breaks In* 87).

Angela Thirkell's novels, like Barbara Pym's unpublished wartime novels and E. M. Delafield's Provincial Lady ones, document the great chaos in England caused by the British government's 1939 policy on evacuees, which created new communities of women. The largest group of evacuees were children sent out by train from the industrial cities of London, Manchester, or Liverpool (which could expect to be bombed), generally accompanied by their female teachers if they were of school age (most male teachers having been conscripted), and by their mothers if they were under five years old. Because evacuees were billeted according to the number of rooms available in a receiving household, single women who had spare bedrooms took in either three or four children or two children accompanied by a teacher or mother. Married women whose husbands were absent on war work or in the armed forces were similarly situated. Having thus reconfigured the average British household, the war required groups of women and children to share both the responsibilities and the privations of their new home lives. These included dealing with the children's head-lice and bed-wetting, and, above all, providing each other with a secure and stable environment in which to live.

Cheerfulness Breaks In contains the most detail about the ways the various women of Barsetshire cope with their obligations. Some, like Mrs. Brandon, make private arrangements and secure delightful babies and their nurse and teachers. Others confront the issue in different ways: the wonderful Mrs. Miller, formerly Miss Morris, who having put up with Aunt Cissie Brandon can surely deal with evacuees, organizes the East End children billeted at Pomfret Madrigal. She puts them with cottagers, as being more suitable to their class than with the residents of the great houses, since the cottagers can use the money allotted by the government to those housing evacuees, and the little evacuees fit right into the dirty, cheerful, crowded environment provided by families like the Thatchers and their "children of shame."

Although Thirkell makes many references to the fact that the evacuee children smell and are impossibly greedy and ill-mannered, the women of Barsetshire rally round to make them clothes, serve them food at the communal kitchen, provide them a Christmas party and presents, and work for their happiness and welfare. The Barsetshire women strive for normality in the new topsy-turvey world, and serve the country and Barsetshire by doing their very best on the home front.

There are many more examples of Thirkell's feelings about the roles of women during the war, but in the end her view of their domestic heroism can be summed up in a single quotation which is alive with colorful and true observations, and which shows how strongly Thirkell felt about her presentation, as her rhetoric builds up a picture of women's wartime work, both official and unofficial:

[A]ll the housewives of England . . . had been working for sixteen or seventeen hours a day ever since the war began, looking after children and aged relatives, standing in queues, walking a mile to the bus and taking an hour to get to the nearest town only to find that the whelk oil or chuckerberry juice or whatever it was that they were told that their children must have wasn't in and it was two hours before the bus went back and anyway they had been given the wrong certificate, slaving at the W.V.S in their meager spare time, suffering evacuees, taking in lodgers because their husband was only getting army pay now, cooking for everyone, fire-watching, being wardens, being mostly too tired to eat, seeing Italian or German prisoners of war riding happily about the country in motor lorries while they pounded along on bicycles against wind and rain or lugged heavy baskets on foot, seeing mountains of coal and coke at the prisoner of war camps while they were down to two hot baths a week and very little soap for the washing and the laundry only coming irregularly every three weeks, seeing Mixo-Lydian and other refugees throwing whole loaves into the pig bin and getting the best cuts at the butcher's, keeping their children nicely dressed while they got shabbier themselves everyday, too driven to consider their looks, unable to have their houses properly cleaned and repaired, having to be servile to tradesmen . . . in a state of permanent tiredness varied by waves of complete exhaustion, yet never letting anyone down dependent on them; this great, valiant, unrecognized class, the stay of domestic England. . . . (*Peace Breaks Out* 284-285)

As the war ends, it is clear that Barsetshire will never be the same. As a champion of the old ways, of the decorum of her county families, and of the rural peace of her fictional county, Thirkell uses the war and its effects as harbingers of change. Her novels celebrate the courage of women in the face of great upheaval, and her fiction in these seven books is significant war fiction, even though it never describes a battle.

Works Cited

Austen, Jane. *Pride and Prejudice*. New York, Bantam, 1983 (orig. 1813).

Calder, Angus. *The Myth of the Blitz*. London: Pimlico, 1991.

Delafield, E. M. *The Provincial Lady in Wartime*. Chicago: Academy of Chicago Publishers, 1986 (orig. 1940).

Gibbons, Stella. *Cold Comfort Farm*. New York: Viking, 1977 (orig. 1932).

Inchfawn, Fay. *Salute to the Village*. London: Lutterworth Press, 1944.

Mackay, Robert. *The Test of War: Inside Britain 1939-45*. London: UCL P, 1991.

Thackeray, William. *Vanity Fair*. London: Penguin, 2003 (orig. 1848).

Thirkell, Angela. *Cheerfulness Breaks In*. Wakefield, Rhode Island and London: Moyer Bell, 1996 (orig. 1940).

Thirkell, Angela. *Growing Up*. Wakefield, Rhode Island and London: Moyer Bell, 1996 (orig. 1943).

Thirkell, Angela. *The Headmistress*. Wakefield, Rhode Island and London: Moyer Bell, 1995 (orig. 1944).

Thirkell, Angela. *Marling Hall*. New York: Carroll & Graf, 1997 (orig. 1942).

Thirkell, Angela. *Miss Bunting*. Wakefield, Rhode Island and London: Moyer Bell, 1996 (orig. 1945).

Thirkell, Angela. *Northbridge Rectory*. New York: Carroll and Graf, 1997 (orig. 1941).

Thirkell, Angela. *Peace Breaks Out*. Wakefield, Rhode Island and London: Moyer Bell, 1997 (orig.1946).

Thirkell, Angela. *Summer Half*. New York: Carroll and Graf, 1991 (orig. 1937).

Contributor

Helen Clare Taylor earned degrees in English at Durham University in England (B. A.), Clark University (M. A.), and the University of Connecticut (Ph. D.). She has published on various twentieth century woman authors. Her most recent publications are "Love and Learning: Barbara Pym and the Romance of the Library" in *All This Reading: The Literary World of Barbara Pym*, edited by Elisabeth Frauke Lenckos and Ellen Miller; "Villainy and the Life of the Mind in A. S. Byatt and Dorothy L. Sayers" in *The Devil Himself: Villainy in Detective Fiction and Film* edited by Stacy Gillis and Philippa Gates; and "A. S. Byatt's *Possession*" in *The Booker Prize*, edited by Merritt Moseley. Dr. Taylor just received a Special Humanities Award for Services to the Humanities from the Louisiana Endowment for the Humanities, and she hosts and produces a weekly radio show on the local Public Radio network (covering three states) which features arts and cultural programming. She is a Professor of English at Louisiana State University in Shreveport, where she teaches Medieval Literature and Literature by Women.

Index

(not including Angela Thirkell, Barsetshire, England, Britain)